The Amazing Adventures of Ben and Gary

Stories of Surfing, Girls, and Growing Up

Ray Bayliss

Contents

The Speech for the Defence

Set in the 1960s and 1970s, and narrated by nineteen-year-old Ben, these are the stories of two ordinary, naïve, and often hapless post-pubescent teenagers who grew up in a small suburb of Perth in Western Australia.

The two mates met at high school and immediately gelled to become close friends. They shared a mutual passion for surfing, and their many adventures together cemented this bond.

This collection of short stories touches on their love of surfing which, along with their travel exploits in search of 'perfect waves', shaped the people they were to become. These important influences were, however, often overshadowed by life's growing pains and the ever-present quest to lose their virginity that bubbled beneath the surface of almost every waking hour.

In this quest, Ben and Gary represent most similar-aged teenagers in that far-off era—always seeking but rarely finding—and I'm sure that many of us will remember those times and readily relate to their journey.

I apologise in advance for the frequent flashbacks from Ben's meandering mind and for the far-fetched events imagined here, as well as the cheesy end-of-story punchlines.

Although not in strict chronological order and mostly pure fiction, the places they visit are certainly real enough and, here and there in each story, a few factual incidents and grains of truth—which usually inspired the tall tales—are sprinkled in amongst the fantasy. Guessing which is which is in your hands!

I hope that you enjoy their amazing adventures and even manage to crack the odd smile or two at their antics.

Just a Bit of Wax

"I'm sorry officer, what did I do wrong?" was the only thing that I could think to say, knowing full well he'd pulled me over for speeding through an amber light. Or was it red? Well, I was on an important mission, wasn't I?

"Driver's license, please!" was his curt reply as my heart sank. I knew this wasn't going to end well.

It all started earlier that day you see, at my best friend's wedding.

Gary Truman has been my best friend since we met in the first year of high school. We grew up together, learned to surf together, and shared our first board—a nine-foot Cordingley that we picked up at a garage sale. It was like a patchwork quilt by the time we'd fixed all the dings but, boy, did we love it!

We stuck together through thick and thin and shared too

many adventures to count, including the east coast 'Surf Pilgrimage' all the way up to Noosa, and many trips to distant and exotic points on the planet in search of perfect waves. We even shared our first legal beer.

At twelve years old, we met on the first day at our new high school. Gary had just moved into the same area that we lived in, and we both ended up at Kelmscott Grammar School, a boys-only institution, something of a rarity for a working- class suburb. I don't know about Gary, but my parents said it would be better for me. No distractions with the girls, I guess, but little did they know!

We sat next to each other on the first day and we were both immediately intimidated by Mrs Dobson, our class teacher, who we would see every morning for roll call, and who taught us English Literature. Well, at least she tried to.

She was a large woman whose appearance helped to keep her flock of misfits on edge. She tied her hair back so tightly from her chubby face that her eyebrows were arched as if she was permanently surprised, and her ears stuck out like Mrs Potato Head. Very scary.

She had a penchant for wearing low-cut tops, and she insisted on wearing ones that were clearly a size or two too small. "Like two bowling balls in a slingshot," said Gary. Had a way with words did my new mate GT.

More like a prison warder than a teacher, she didn't use a truncheon thankfully, but she did have a heavy two-foot wooden ruler instead. She would slap it against her ample thigh or her other hand when she wanted to make a point or, more often, to recapture your attention when your mind had wandered from the works of Shakespeare or Tennyson, as mine often did. I'm sure it must have hurt her because she'd slap harder and harder if you didn't immediately listen. You could just imagine her rattling it along the bars of the cells to intimidate even the most hardened criminals.

As we quickly found out, it didn't take long for her to spot our aimless doodlings or, even worse, heavy eyelids, at which point she'd whack the ruler down on the desktop. This would make us jump out of our skin and cause the whole desk to bounce and shudder, scattering our stuff all over the classroom floor.

She never did hit anyone with it, not that I can recall anyway. It was the threat of that ruler that scared the hell out of us and kept us all more or less in line.

Right from the start though, Gary was the class comedian, and I think it was a family thing. He told me that his dad did a stand-up routine at the local working men's club most Saturday nights, in the days when comedians didn't need to 'F and Blind' to get a laugh. Mr Truman was hilarious, and he didn't seem to be like most other parents—you know, super strict and absolute killjoys. He just had a way to pull us into line without the usual shouting and threats, even when dealing out a dose of discipline. A very clever man.

Gary was a natural too, it must have been in his genes.

On that very first day at school, he had me and the rest of the class in stitches at the expense of an unwitting Mrs

Dobson.

After only one warning, she brought the ruler down on Gary's desktop with an almighty crash. He screamed and fell to the floor like a rag doll, covering his face with both hands, his body convulsing as he continued to wail.

Visibly distraught and ever so slightly panicked, Mrs Dobson scooped him up and pulled his face into her ample breasts. "Oh, dear boy, are you alright? I didn't mean to..."

Gary, taking full advantage of this rare opportunity to enjoy such a handsome cleavage, let out a few squeaks and whimpers whilst nuzzling further into boobie heaven. This only seemed to make her squeeze him in tighter and tighter, and when his head finally emerged from its soft, pink Valhalla, he turned to the class and, with crossed eyes and cheeks sucked in, he let out a long, contented groan.

"Oh, you're alright... I'm so relieved... good boy," stuttered Mrs Dobson as Gary stood up and returned to his seat. The rest of us, tears streaming down our faces, were bursting at the seams trying not to laugh out loud.

That was it! Gary had cemented his place in school folklore and, of course, the story grew ever more fantastic as it was told and retold. His reputation grew further as he performed more comic capers around school whenever opportunity knocked.

Always sailing close to the wind, he even managed to squeeze a wry smile out of Mr Bradley, the science teacher who, I swear, was a dead ringer for Lurch in the Addams Family.

"Sir, if sound can't travel through a vacuum, then why is Mum's Hoover so loud?" said Gary with a quizzical look on his face. Luckily, he managed to dodge the blackboard duster that Mr B flung at him. He was normally extremely accurate with the wooden missile and so I guessed that he probably intended to miss.

Gazza finally went too far when, to avoid a cross-country run on a particularly cold and rainy day, he feigned a severe stomach ache in the change rooms. The medical pantomime took an unexpected turn when his bluff was called, and he was promptly whisked off to the local hospital by the Deputy Headmaster, Mr Cash.

He was a class act, was our Gary, and under the suspicious and watchful eye of 'Killer Cash' (as he was known to his frightened horde back at school), he was still in full flow as he continued the ruse in the Emergency Department. Well, he had to, didn't he?

Flustered by the crocodile tears and the screams whenever he touched Gary's middle, and intimidated by the impatient grunts of Mr Cash, the attending junior doctor diagnosed acute appendicitis and admitted the class clown to the hospital there and then.

Gary was operated on within the hour.

Three weeks later, minus his perfectly healthy appendix, looking pale and just a touch sheepish, he arrived back at school with a new and very clear sense of where he should draw the line.

Anyway, I digress. Back to the wedding.

Naturally, I was Gary's Best Man, and everything was going swimmingly until, holding out his hymn book, the vicar asked for the rings. No, I hadn't forgotten them—give me some credit, won't you!

I'd slipped them into my pocket for safe keeping, along with a block of my surf wax—something I carried with me wherever I went and whatever I was wearing.

You see, a block of wax is a sort of universal currency amongst surfers. Sometimes you give it away for free and, as a result, gain brownie points with a scary-looking local, or break it in half to offer to another surfer, making a friend for life. Other times it can be exchanged for, well, almost anything if the other dude is desperate enough for a surf and his board happens to be bare. Difficult for 'straights' to understand I know but, trust me, a smart surfer never leaves home without it.

Now, where was I? Oh yes, the rings.

I had the rings tucked away safely with the wax which was my amateur home-made recipe. I'd been making my own for a few weeks, and I used candles, beeswax, and vanilla oil which gives it a great smell. Getting it just right is a bit of an art, but my wax was usually pretty good, even though I say so myself.

But not today.

It was swelteringly hot, and we'd been standing in the sun for the best part of an hour before we got into the church, and this was only minutes before the bride arrived and the organist struck up the Wedding March. So, wouldn't you know it, the wax had melted—too much oil again, damn it! It can be a bit hit and miss, you see, but when perfected, it saves you fifty cents a block!

So, what I had in my pocket was a warm, gooey, albeit sweet-smelling, mess, and somewhere in there were the two bands of gold. These were now well mixed with the contents of a packet of Wrigley's, a couple of loose durries, and one (unused) condom. You see, it was my first time as Best Man, and I'd heard that the main benefit of this important role was that you were often seduced by one of the bridesmaids, and I didn't want to be caught short now, did I?

The look on the bride's face was a picture of pure horror when I offered up a handful of the aforementioned semi-liquid cocktail. She was not happy, and neither was the vicar, who now had the stuff oozing all over his open hymn book. At least the rings were there, though.

What really put the cap on it was Gary's dad.

Sitting in the front row, he'd seen everything and started giggling. Not just a discreet titter, no, he was soon almost crying and couldn't stop himself descending into a loud belly laugh that echoed through the cloisters.

Well, this set me off, and then Gary, who doubled over laughing, which was a big mistake because he let out a loud fart, a result of the Emu Bitter he'd consumed earlier as a bit of Dutch Courage.

I did warn him, but he never listens.

Marlene, the bride, screamed and lashed out at the now guffawing Gary. She didn't time her swing very well and Gary managed to duck out of harm's way but, tragically, the vicar didn't. Marlene packed quite a punch when she wanted to, and so the Reverend went down like a sack of potatoes.

Seizing her chance, Miss Richardson, the bespectacled and silver-haired organist, leapt from her seat and started giving mouth-to-mouth to the now groaning vicar. Her eyes were filled with passion, and writhing with ecstasy, she now groaned too. The vicar's eyes opened wide and bulged from their sockets as he fought for air. Temporarily suffocated by his would-be-lover's embrace, he slumped back to the floor, unconscious.

Luckily, Gary's mum had some smelling salts in her handbag. Apparently, she always carried them because Granny Truman had a habit of fainting at the slightest provocation. Very strange. Interestingly, she didn't pass out on this occasion but, rather, she was now on her feet shouting obscenities. I'm not sure why, or who they were aimed at, but it was pretty colourful, I can tell you!

Anyway, sensing that he needed to intervene before the randy organist went a little *too* far in her love quest, the choirmaster entered the fray and dragged her off the vicar, who was eventually revived, the rings extricated from the still-sticky wax, Marlene was calmed sufficiently to carry on, and Gary composed just enough to say, "With this ring...".

I could see that I needed to stay well away from Marlene at

the reception and so I gave my speech from a safe distance, and I left out a few of the more edgy stories about her new husband. Things settled down, and even the bride's mum, Mrs Cardiff, stopped scowling at me for a while.

The wedding meal and several Swan lagers later, the DJ started playing some good old Aussie rock and, after a bit of solo head banging, I was dragged onto the dancefloor by the Matron of Honour, the bride's sister Debbie who, by the way, was smoking hot. Well, I thought she was, and she seemed to be really into me, unlike my last girlfriend, Josie Pinbury. Anyway, she was all over me like a rash, and that made her completely irresistible.

We drank and chatted and drank some more and, as the night went on and the guests thinned out, we had the dancefloor almost to ourselves. The DJ slowed things down and played some Marvin Gaye, which seemed to drive Debbie wild.

At one point, she had her hand down the front of my trousers, and I was trying to hop away to avoid Gary's gran fainting. Granny Truman had managed to haul herself up onto the dancefloor and was dancing the 'Nutbush' on her own. Not in time to Marvin obviously, and so I guess it was Tina that was playing in her head.

"Let's go to the beach," Debbie whispered in a low, sexy voice. "Won't it be a bit dark?" I *almost* said before the penny dropped.

"Sure thing, babe," I said, conjuring up my best, deep Sean Connery voice, but then I froze as panic set in.

My one and only condom was still stuck fast to Psalm 23 and probably now safely ensconced in the church vestry.

My brain was racing (as was my pulse), and I persuaded Debbie to go to freshen up before we left for our, hopefully, passionate triste, and I bolted for my trusty panel van.

The thing was, you see, I'd had many false starts before, and something always managed to mess things up. But not this time, tonight was the night!

I knew there was a late-night servo a mile or two up the highway, and so I set off like a bat out of hell, desperately hoping that the vending machine was still there and well-stocked. I'd bought the now-missing condom from there a couple of years before, when I was going to another mate's bucks night. Typical wishful thinking, I guess.

I was flying along when I saw the blue lights in my rear-view mirror and heard the siren.

"Have you been drinking?" said the now increasingly irritated police officer, snapping me out of my reminiscences. Given that the van smelled like a brewery, I suppose he didn't have to be a super sleuth.

At least he didn't have a breathalyser, which were still fairly rare, and I managed a reasonable job of walking the line with my eyes closed and whilst touching my nose. Well, I thought I did but, apparently, he didn't. So, I spent the next three hours in Perth Watch House waiting for my dad to collect me. That meeting was going to be real fun.

Therefore, for a while at least, my virginity stayed intact.

Debbie never really spoke to me again and would scowl at me whenever we bumped into each other. Apparently, Gary, drunk but not *that* drunk and, most likely, with revenge on his mind for the rings debacle, had told her that I'd got tired of waiting and had sneaked off to the beach with one of the other bridesmaids. For good measure, he told Debbie that I'd said that my new love interest was sexier and much better looking than her. Thanks, mate!

Oh, how cruel he could be sometimes—and all because of Just a Bit of Wax!

Surfers Can Fly

"Tampilang paspor sametoné. Paspor!" screamed the immigration officer. No matter how many times he repeated it, I still didn't understand a word. I've never been good with languages.

They had dragged me and Gary into a small, windowless room, and Gazza was having the same trouble as me. "No understandee. No understandee. Me Oss-tray-lee-an!" he shouted repeatedly, and ever louder.

The room was tiny, and the only light came from a single globe that hung from the ceiling on a short cord. The place smelled of sweat, and I wasn't sure if that was me, Gary, or our captor. I had not showered for at least three days but relied on the cleansing action of the Badung Straits. I had a quick sniff at my armpit, and yes, it was me. I don't know why, but they are sometimes a bit of a mystery and, when I least need it, they can smell like a footy player's jock strap.

It was Josie Pinbury, my girlfriend at the time, that first pointed it out to me, and not very delicately, I must say. "Bloody hell, Ben, you smell like a bull that's just serviced a paddock full of cows!" Such a poet was Josie. But perhaps that's why we never, you know, did it—even after I discovered Brut for Men, the very latest in man scent.

It wasn't for the want of trying, mind, and of course, we did our fair share of heavy petting.

I remember our last date, the one that put the final nail in the coffin, so to speak. We were at the drive-in at Scarborough watching er, hum, well, I can't actually remember what we were watching because we didn't see any of the movie as it turned out. Josie wasn't a small girl, and she wore short mini-skirts and stockings, complete with a suspender belt. Maybe not the best look, but it was fine by me and my overheated hormones!

It took us about five minutes of watching the movie trailers before we could hold ourselves no longer and so we scrambled from the front seats into the back of my panel van. A few weeks earlier, and in anticipation of what might lie ahead in my jet-set lifestyle, I'd added a thin foam mattress to cover the metal floor, and we rolled around on it in rushed, noisy passion.

Unfortunately, things went downhill fast.

She had no trouble undoing my jeans but, as I struggled to find my way up her tight skirt, I pushed and pulled at her stockings a bit too desperately. Tragedy struck when one of the buttons on her suspender belt broke free from its elastic anchorage and catapulted skywards like a bullet. It ricocheted off the metal roof of the van and struck Josie square in the middle of her forehead and with such force that it almost knocked her out.

It wouldn't have been so bad, but it took about two weeks for the swelling to go down and another week for the distinctive shape of the button and the buttonholes, all now a lovely blue colour, to start to fade. You could still see it at Christmas.

Needless to say, Josie wasn't impressed, and that was the last time I saw her. I did see her brother, Lenny, about a week later and, enthusiastically, he insisted on buying me a pint. With a broad grin, he told me that Josie copped hell from their mum, who must have identified the missile from its near photo-perfect impression on her forehead, and she had grounded poor Josie for a month. Clearly no love lost between those siblings!

Anyway, back to our predicament with immigration.

We'd been surfing Bali for almost a week before we met the Martin brothers, Dave and Ned, two Americans on their first trip to the 'Island of the Gods'. These guys were the business. Shoulder-length blonde hair, beautiful matching Hobie boards, cool surf shorts, Levi jeans, Huarache sandals, bitchin' accents, and they were from So Cal for Heaven's sake! Wherever that was. Seppos, my dad used to call them, short for Septic Tanks, his rhyming slang for Yanks. Strange man, my dad.

And they had dope.

You see, as cool as me and Gary were—except for our

clothes of course; and our hair, which was still more or less short back and sides because of our jobs; and our boards, which were battered and sun yellowed; or our grungy singlets; and our wafer-thin thongs—we had never, and I mean never, tried dope. Not that we hadn't actually *seen* it before, but it wasn't exactly common in sleepy little Kelmscott, WA.

At first, we refused and stuck to several Bintangs as our regular evening anaesthetic, but as the holiday wore on, the Yanks got more and more insistent. We didn't really understand why, but it seemed to have become a challenge for them to get us stoned.

Gary was the first to relent, quickly followed by me around thirty seconds later.

We'd just dragged ourselves back up the beach after our first outing at Ulus (or Uluwatu to the less well-travelled amongst you), and after we'd spent what felt like forever battling to get back in.

We were out of our depth, literally and figuratively, because today this really was an expert break, on a day for experts, and when even experts were getting obliterated, expertly. Get the picture? We were pretty good surfers and could tackle a fair-sized Yallingup, or even Margaret River on the right day but this was at a different level.

We had both managed to get out the back and, within half an hour or so, we'd each scored a couple of nice, but ever-so-slightly-scary head-and-a-half high waves. Then we noticed we were sitting on our own. Everyone else had paddled towards the horizon and were still heading out.

"They're dickheads, Ben, don't worry, we'll be fine," said Gary. Now Gary has always been a better surfer than me, but he can be a bit reckless sometimes and so, no, I wasn't reassured.

I did warn him, but he never listens.

Two minutes after the 'dickheads' had comfortably settled about two hundred metres further out, a monster set blocked out much of the remaining sunlight. I screamed something and I suspect that my coach and mentor, Gary, shat himself because there was a new and strange colour in the water around him. We thrashed around and started to paddle out, heading for where we thought the shoulder of the first monster would be. As it turned out, it didn't matter because, as we climbed up the face of the first huge wave, desperately scratching for the lip, the mountain of water started to spill and then quickly crashed, throwing us both backwards over the falls. Anyone who has experienced such a treat will know how utterly helpless you become within a split second.

After a pounding to end all poundings from wave after wave and being repeatedly held down in the resulting washing machine for what seemed like an eternity, we finally made it back to the beach. Our two American mates rushed over shouting words of concern and support like, "Are you kooks freakin' crazy? Didn't you see that set coming? Where did you think everyone was going? For a deep-water piss? What were you assholes thinking?"

Now 'crazy' I could take, even 'assholes', but 'kooks'? Back home he'd have got a black eye over that insult! But I was battered and bruised and shagged out after the near drowning and, if I'm honest, I knew full well that he was bigger and stronger and would have probably beat the crap out of me. So, I shrugged my shoulders and offered up a weak smile.

Gary finally broke the tension and said, "Got any dope on you?"

So that was our first time, sitting at the base of the cliffs at Uluwatu, watching the sun set over the now steadily dropping swell lines (hmm, timing is everything, right?), with our newfound friends who, as it turned out, as well as being surfers and dope heads, were also accomplished thieves.

They stole stuff all the time and bragged about it to anyone and everyone who would listen. Cigarettes, T-shirts, beer from the little store opposite Kuta beach, in fact just about anything they could get their hands on. Being barefaced was their modus operandi, they explained. One would create a distraction, and the other would pick up the target item and walk off. Worked every time they said.

"Not cool, not cool at all," said Gary as we headed back to our digs. Of course we didn't join their criminal enterprise, but Gazza was right and, with hindsight, we should have followed our gut instinct and stayed well clear of them.

The first time we saw them in action and, as it turned out, the last, was back in Kuta.

Me and Gary were staying in a Losmen, not far from Poppies, a fairly new little restaurant on a dirt lane off the main street, and we arranged to meet the Yanks there for a beer and food. They hadn't been before, and so we were in the driving seat for a change. Score one for the Aussies!

After the obligatory round or two of Bintangs, we all ordered the staple surfer's dinner, Nasi Goreng, which filled the considerable gap left after a full day in the surf. We all wolfed down the delicious and aromatic dish in a flash, and then Gary went to the bar to order another round of beers, whilst I nipped to the dunny. As I came out and joined Gary at the bar, our newfound mates shouted something and then bolted up the street, laughing and hooting.

A couple of staff gave chase but were no match for the practiced sprinters, and so their attention turned to us. It cost us six dollars to cover their bill too, which was only four bucks short of clearing us out! Fuming, we picked up our backpacks and left.

We eventually caught up with Dave and Ned down by the beach and demanded our money back, but to no avail. They just stared us down and said that we were stupid for not running too. We later discovered that this was their favourite party trick to score free food, and they were fast running out of places and people to scam.

Thieving bastards.

We didn't see them again; they sort of disappeared, and for our last couple of days, we scraped by on noodles from a street vendor and begged the odd beer and ciggie from fellow travellers.

And so it was that we finally arrived at the airport for our flight home to Perth, sunburned, surfed out, and hungry, but with that stoked feeling that only surfers know and understand.

Queuing to go through immigration, we bumped into a few other like-minded souls who were on their way home too. Funnily enough, they all seemed to know Dave and Ned, and most had been on the receiving end of one or other of their scams.

Such as Rod, for example, an angry-looking guy from Balga with no front teeth.

Apparently, he was a glassie at his local pub and had to eject a particularly nasty patron who had just been refused at the bar. In drunken protest, the bloke had promptly whipped out his weaner and pissed all over Rod's shoes.

Well, apparently, they were Rod's pride and joy, being almost brand-new DBs, or desert boots for those readers who must have missed the nineteen sixties and seventies. Well, DBs weren't cheap but were the 'must have' for any self-respecting surfer, and so Rod was not a happy chappy at this point. He promptly head-butted the offending patron and then proceeded to beat the shit out of him. Even though the guy was drunk, he still managed to get a couple of punches in, including a lucky one with a heavy ashtray that claimed Rod's front teeth.

Calm was restored when the offender was thrown out but, apparently, Rod's DBs always had a bit of an odour, particularly when he was on the dance floor on a hot summer night at Pinocchio's in the city. His mates learned not to mention it as it usually sent him into a bit of a rant, and no one was quite sure where it might end.

Anyway, I digress. The long and the short of it was that our American friend Dave picked the wrong guy to scam. Rod caught him nicking cash from his bag on the beach and so gave him a pasting that he won't forget. Well, that's the story we heard, anyway.

We shuffled our way forward in the long line, inching closer to the front when Gary, rummaging in his backpack, let out a yelp. He had a look of horror on his face—a bit like the time he trapped his wotsit in his zip.

"My bloody passport's gone!" he screamed in panic. Three seconds later I discovered the same.

"Those damn Yanks must have stolen our passports!" I offered in explanation to the immigration officer when I finally understood what he was screaming at me.

It was a long couple of hours, I can tell you, whilst he made several calls to the Australian Consulate in Denpasar. After contacting our parents and checking our birth records, they eventually came back to him and confirmed that we were indeed who we said we were and gave the OK for us to get back home. Phew!

Escorted by two immigration officials, we ran down to where the plane was waiting to depart. Our boarding cards in hand we scaled the steps only to be met by a stewardess wanting to see our passports before letting us on board.

The drama thankfully ended after my uniformed

immigration friend shouted those sweet words from the tarmac, "Surfers Can fly, Surfers Can Fly."

Take Your Turn in the Line-up

"Toma tu turno en la alineacion!" said the angry local.

"She's not very friendly," said Gary, stating the obvious as usual.

I should have listened to my dad in the first place, but I guess I'd have never gone anywhere if I did.

"I'm tellin ya, it'll nevva happin', ya great lanky puddn'," were the best words of encouragement that my dad could offer when I told him that me and Gary planned to head off and travel the world in search of perfect waves.

"Awaye man, ya've bin watching too minny of them bluddy surf movies, ya stupad dimentid cocker."

If any of you need that translating, then please just let me know.

You see, my dad is a Pom from Newcastle way — "Geordie Land" he calls it. "Wye aye man, it's God's Own Country is what it is," he often laments with a misty, faraway look in his eyes.

We were Ten Pound Poms, and I was only four when we arrived with Mum, Dad, and my older brother, Gerry. We were settled in Perth—well, on the outskirts in a place called Gosnells. Not much there at the time, just a few new subdivisions, some shops, a deli, fuel station and, of course a pub. At first, we lived in a hostel with five other migrant families. "Like a bluddy prison an' all," dad would say in his letters home. Mum, of course, got us through it, and we were soon renting a place of our own just up the road in Kelmscott. "Much nicer here," said mum. "It's got a church." Not that she had time to go much.

So, I suppose I'm a Pom really, although no one would know it.

"Bi proud of it, man," Dad would chant with his chest puffed out. "Yer a Pom thru an' thru. Al'as respect Her Majesty and ya muther country, that's where yez from an' dun't ya forgit it!"

Thanks for the advice, Dad.

But primary school in Gosnells and Kelmscott High School for Boys made sure that I was a Dinkie Die Aussie, and so, I'm sorry your Majesty!

Anyway, enough of the family history.

Me and Gary had talked loads of times about heading off on our 'Magical Mystery Tour' to search for endless waves, but we had never plucked up the courage to do it.

Then came the incident with the twin sisters, the police officer, and the fire engine.

It all started when we'd come back from Yallingup after a week of great surf. Main break was a perfect three to four-foot, and Indijup Point provided the fall-back when Yalls topped eight-foot on a couple of days later in the week, which sent us scuttling for waves more suited to our nervous dispositions.

Full of stoke after a good week away, we decided that Saturday night would be spent at Pinocchio's looking for the next loves of our lives—well any girls that would at least dance with us. Our track record wasn't what you'd call great, but if points were awarded for trying, then we'd be top of the table.

Replete in our platform-soled shoes, flares, and tight-fitting flowered shirts, and on the right side of several Swan Lagers, we hit the dancefloor on our weekly quest to attract the girls. Girls who were going to fall for our good looks and obvious 'cool'. Girls who would hang off our every word and who would finally end our seemingly lifelong quest. We were both eighteen and still virgins for heaven's sake!

Not that there hadn't been chances, lots of *chances* and we came close, of course, tantalisingly close—even if this was just in our naïve, befuddled heads. Basically, we were clueless and just plain scared when things got close to the crunch.

Our education in this department had been fairly typical of the time. Basically, it was woeful. A few anatomy diagrams in our biology books, the mating habits of blue whales explained by a young, newly minted female teacher, and the odd erotic magazine shared behind the change rooms at school. And, if you were really unlucky, you might get an embarrassing two-minute briefing from your dad. Yep, woeful is the word.

And then there was Mrs White.

I was just fifteen, and on Saturday mornings I used to clean swimming pools for a couple of neighbours, which helped add a few extra dollars to my pocket money.

The Whites were a new family that had moved in next door to us and, luckily, I managed to add them to my client list. I put them first on my rounds but, like all good teenagers, my weekends were the time for a good lie-in, and so it was around eleven thirty when I knocked on their door. No one seemed to be home, and so I went through the side gate and into the pool yard. Mr White had shown me where the equipment was kept, and so I collected the leaf scoop and, whistling away, I headed through the leafy garden that surrounded the pool.

I wasn't really concentrating because I tripped over a sun lounger and fell flat on my face.

"Are you okay?" a woman's voice chirped over the noise of the pool pump as I got up.

I spun around to see that Mrs White was lying on the lounger sunbaking but, more than that, she was stark naked! My heart leapt up to my throat as I stared at her. She was old, you know, about thirty I estimated, but with a gorgeous, slim, and sun-tanned body. Yikes, had I won Lotto?

I had never seen naked breasts or 'down there' in the flesh before, and so I stood there open-mouthed and unable to reply to her question. These days it's a regular sight in those foreign movies on the telly, but all I knew back then was that it was an awesome sight to behold.

I was wearing last season's footy shorts, which were a tad too small for me, and so, with all those hormones flooding my bloodstream, it didn't take long for my admiration for her body to become pretty obvious.

I grabbed a footstool and held it tight in front of my rapidly bulging shorts. Mrs White, clearly revelling in my acute embarrassment, chuckled and said, "You must be Ben from next door. I hope I won't be in your way…" I mumbled a bumbling reply as I backed away, unable to take my eyes off her.

By this time, I was sweating and wondering what I should do and, as my arousal grew to bursting point, my wedding tackle slipped out of my undersized shorts. Panicked, I pulled the stool tighter into my crotch, pretending it was heavier than it was.

This was a big mistake, which I only found out when I eventually stopped staring at Mrs White's beautiful breasts and turned towards the pool. I tried to put the stool down but my rock-hard 'meat and two veg' were stuck through the hand hole in the top of the damn thing. I let out a squeal as I tried repeatedly to pull free and then everything went sort of hazy.

As it happened, Mrs White said she knew what to do and so, half an hour later and with the help of the best part of a bottle of olive oil, I was freed from the cruel and painful trap. At least she didn't have to call the Fire Brigade thank goodness.

Despite her skill and gentle touch, which in different circumstances would have made for a completely different story, it took over a week for the swelling to go down and, another week for the bruising to fade. The pain and embarrassment stayed with me for some time, as did the memory of that naked body.

I still flinch every time I see one of those bloody stools, but they do carry some pretty nice background pictures for my dreams.

And so ended my first-hand education on women's anatomy which, although extremely enjoyable and enlightening at the time, did nothing to prepare me for what to do later in life when in a heated and passionate moment and faced with the critical 'crunch time'.

Anyway, back to Pinocchio's.

After a few acrobatic disco numbers on the dancefloor which had only attracted the attention of a particularly grumpy bouncer, we decided to slink back to the bar for another dose of Dutch Courage.

Standing in our usual spot, I wondered if I'd had too much to drink because walking towards us was this stunning girl, but in duplicate. There seemed to be two of them. There *were* two of them! Virtually identical twins and heading straight for us, both smiling. What the...?

I shot a quick look behind me to see if they were really looking for someone else but, no, there was no one there. It must be us!

The rest of the night was a blur of dancing, laughing, drinking, and more drinking. Tracey was the twin that was my new-found love, and Julie clearly had the hots for Gary.

Then came kissing and groping in the dark corner that we'd scouted many times before, and which we knew would give us some privacy should we ever get any girls remotely interested in us. We'd finally, *finally* made it to our fabled 'Corner'. Things were looking up at last!

It was around two am when we spilled out onto Murray Street, laughing and screeching and, off balance yet again, I managed to fall headlong at the feet of a patrolling cop.

As I drunkenly used his trousers to climb myself up off the ground, he grabbed me by the hair and hauled me upright. "Hey!" was the only word that I managed to utter before he slapped me across the face, just hard enough to snap me back to full compos mentis without knocking me out.

"What's your name, sonny?" he growled through clenched teeth.

"Robinson, Ben Robinson," I blurted. Well, I was drunk

and didn't think to lie, did I?

"Get yourself home, mister Robinson, before I change my mind and put you behind bars for the night!" he shouted as the others stood silently looking on, pretending not to know me.

Momentarily sober, I mumbled an apology, and as the constable walked away, Gary and the girls dragged me off to the safety of the car park opposite. The twins each produced a half-bottle of whisky from their handbags and so it didn't take us long to see the funny side of the incident.

That's when we spotted the fire engine.

It was sitting there in the far corner with no one around and, for some unknown reason, it was unlocked. Drunk and giggling, Tracey and I climbed in the front seat, and Gary and Julie climbed in the crew seat behind.

The grunts and groans from the back suggested that old Gazza was getting well past 'First Base', and I wasn't doing too badly either.

Tracey was hot, and I mean hot, and certainly knew her way around a passion session in a parked vehicle. She was writhing about as we kissed and, to my amazement, after slipping out of her blouse, she managed to unclip and remove her bra with one hand before tossing it onto the dashboard, and all in about two seconds!

Things were getting pretty steamy and, I have to admit, that I was in danger of letting the horse bolt before the gate had even been opened, if you get my drift. Well, it was my first time (finally...) and so fair's fair. And she was extremely hot.

This was it!

I managed to drunkenly take off my shirt whilst Tracey helped me fumble out of my daks. I then whisked off my Y Fronts with a flourish, just like I'd always imagined I would, and, like a prize stallion, I was all revved up and ready for action! At which point Tracey let out a scream, swung her foot up and kicked me hard in the gonads.

It was me that was screaming now and, clutching my wedding tackle with tears rolling down my face, I fell backwards and my backside hit the dashboard exactly where the button for the siren was located.

"What sort of a girl do you think I am? You, you twisted pervert!" she bellowed over the noise of the siren which, by now, was in full song.

"But, but I, you..." was all I could say through clenched teeth before another wave of pain rendered me mute.

Gary had seen everything from his poll position behind us and was laughing so hard that he peed himself. Too many beers on top of all that passion, I suspect.

I did warn him, but he never listens.

This clearly killed the romance in the back seat and a less-than-amused Julie who, to my surprise and despite all the passionate groaning, was still fully clothed, punched Gary hard in the stomach. This, in his inebriated state, made him drop a poo to go with the pee.

Julie, clearly not happy with the vile scene before her, and of course the stench, started shouting obscenities the like of which I'd not heard outside the changing rooms at our beloved Kenwick Footy Club. She then jumped out of the rear door, closely followed by Tracey, who quickly climbed back into her clothes and leapt from our would-be love nest in the front.

They had to push their way through quite a crowd which, to our surprise, had gathered to see where the fire was.

I scrambled back into my clothes and frantically tried to silence the wailing siren. Unfortunately, in my panic, I hit several buttons and only succeeded in turning on the blue flashing lights to accompany the deafening noise, and goodness knows what else. Well, it was pretty dark, and my eyes were still watering from Tracey's well-aimed assault!

Leaving his wet and soiled underpants behind, Gary grabbed my arm and pulled me from the other side of the now popular attraction, and only seconds before my police officer friend arrived to sort out the chaos. He had to break up a fight that had started over the fire hose, which was gushing water all over the car park, sending the crowd running for higher ground.

As my dad always said, "Some drunks'll feight owver bluddy out!" Seems he's right about that.

Luckily, we were camouflaged by the considerable throng of onlookers and managed to tip-toe away to the safety of the empty street. We then legged it for the train station where we hid in the dunny until the first train to Armadale at six am.

The story made the local TV news the following evening, with a serious looking Acting Sergeant stating that they were looking for two males who, in his words had, "Broken into a parked fire engine and then urinated and defecated all over the crew seats, rendering the vehicle unusable for several days."

Apparently, the delinquents had then set off the emergency siren and blue lights and, even worse, the scumbags pumped the on-board water tank dry of its three thousand litres of water. This had, unfortunately, flooded a nearby kebab shop, causing some damage and a further breach of the peace as the drunken late-night patrons fought for the few remaining doners.

"Must have been one of those other buttons," I later suggested to Gary. "Probably the green one, I bet."

Worse still, the sergeant held up, understandably at arm's length, Gary's underpants, which were now quite stiff and a distinct brownish colour. "If anyone recognises these, then please come forward," said the serious-looking copper. He also had a description and an artist's impression of the two hoodlums who perpetrated this heinous crime.

"That looks like that Nat King Cole," said Mum, pointing to the one on the right. "You know, the singer. Is he in town?"

"He was black, and he's dead, ya daft 'ol moo!" replied Dad

in his usual supportive way.

"He doesn't look black. Maybe it's the telly," was her thoughtful response as she bashed the top of our rented Pye black and white set. I could sort of see the resemblance myself, but I'd learned through bitter experience not to get in between them in an argument.

Like the time they were arguing about TV personality Johnny O'Keefe and whether he wore a wig. All I said was that it was his choice to wear one if he wanted to but, in my opinion, he definitely wore a rug on top. Well, I might as well have called the Pope an atheist, because Mum turned on me and let fly, and then Dad grabbed me by the shirt front and threatened to knock my block off for upsetting Mum. Clearly, Johnny's wig was a sensitive subject, and so I've been strictly Switzerland since then!

Anyway, all that was irrelevant. The point was that me and Gary had to lie low. After all, it might not be long before the copper that I accosted leaving Pinocchio's put two and two together, or Julie and Tracey came forward with vital clues as to our identities. Julie might put in an anonymous call about Gary's jocks and Tracey had probably caught a glimpse of the heart shaped birthmark on my wotsit for example—not something many had seen (unfortunately).

And so it was that we finally decided to empty our savings accounts, quit our jobs, and skip town to embark on our 'Endless Summer' surf odyssey.

"I tell ya, it'll only end in bluddy tears, ya silly pillocks," was my dad's fond farewell.

Those words were ringing in my ears as we stood in the dilapidated police station in Mazatlan, Mexico.

Gary and I had flown there virtually non-stop from Perth via Delhi, Bahrain, London, Bangor Maine, New York, Chicago, Los Angeles and San Diego. It had cost us a big chunk of our travel money and had taken us almost six days to get there, and so we were well and truly knackered.

You see, I'm not sure how we got the idea, but we thought that Mazatlan was one of the stops that the movie maker Bruce Brown, with surfers Robert August and Mike Hynson, had made when they filmed the iconic 1964 surf movie 'The Endless Summer', and we wanted to follow in their footsteps.

There was a long line for immigration at the airport and only one checkpoint desk was open. The official was clearly taking his duties very seriously and scrutinised every person and their passport in minute detail. We were dead on our feet from all the travelling and so, after almost two hours of waiting and mustering all the bravado I could, I pushed Gary forward until we were almost at the front.

"Official business, professional surfers, competition officials!" was all I could think to repeatedly shout as we dragged our slouch bags and boards down the line.

Not surprisingly the crowd didn't buy it, and a scuffle broke out between Gary and one particularly unhappy chap who, it turned out, *was* a professional surfer and *was* here to judge a newly world-ranked contest in Mexico. Just our luck!

The disturbance attracted the attention of a rather big and not very friendly Federale who screamed at us and then pushed us into a poky interview room, before dragging us off to the nearby police station. There he searched us, rubber gloves and all, and he seemed to enjoy the rather intimate event far too much, I have to say. And it would seem that Vaseline wasn't available in Mexico.

Whilst we recovered from the undignified and over-zealous finger rooting, he searched our bags.

Unfortunately, our Spanish was non-existent and so we couldn't seem to get him and his colleagues to understand that the white substance in my luggage was just a bag of washing powder that my mum had insisted I pack. "So you can have clean undies, in case you have to go to hospital," was her matronly and wholly reasonable explanation.

The confusion was finally cleared up when one of the group of police officers watching our interrogation, a particularly large and sweaty cop with red eyes and a purple nose, decided to sneak outside and snort some of the stuff.

He was spitting bubbles for at least an hour before a local medic was summoned to flush out his sinuses with a hosepipe.

Not a pretty sight.

I think it was just to save face that they insisted on deporting us the following day. And so, after spending a particularly uncomfortable night in a cell that we shared with ten others, we arrived back at the airport with an armed guard. He manhandled us both to the check-in desk before taking off the completely unnecessary handcuffs that we'd been fitted with.

"Toma tu turno en la alineacion!" the check-in clerk barked as we shuffled forward to board the plane.

So our 'Endless Summer' dreams would have to wait for another day, and all because we didn't Take Our Turn in the Line-up!

California Dreamin'

It was Gary's idea, really.

You see, we'd just been deported from Mexico over a little 'illicit substance' misunderstanding. They'd put us on a plane to San Diego because that's where we'd arrived from and, as we walked down the steps of the plane, and squinting against the bright sunshine, Gary said, "Hey Ben, let's go to the Bu."

I wasn't sure if he was feeling a bit sick after the flight and so I ignored him.

"The Bu, you know, Malibu," he chirped in a fake American accent.

I thought about it for a minute and was just about to respond when I spotted the immigration officials waiting at the bottom of the steps. "Oh crap, not again!" was my best mate's comment as they called out our names.

After spending another exhausting two hours going over and over the 'white powder' saga in Mazatlan, during which time they took away Mum's washing powder for testing, they finally stamped our passports, and we were on our way.

Not that it wasn't without drama though.

At one point when things were looking a bit bleak and the immigration officer was talking about jail time for importation of illegal drugs, Gary claimed that he hardly knew me, and he agreed that drug mules should be locked up for good. Thanks, mate!

Mind you, that wasn't the first occasion he had denied all knowledge of my being. There was the time we were in Mandurah having a few drinks after a full day surfing Miami Bay, Falcon.

Hot on the heels of my lack of success with Tracey the twin, I had been on fire that night, but without the fire engine this time. The beer had helped of course, and I'd had a shower at the beach—cold but necessary. I'd also covered myself in Brut for Men, just to make sure, and put on my clean jeans and white T-shirt. I was smokin'!

Gary, on the other hand, had skipped the shower and was still in his surf shorts and blue singlet. "Animal attraction," he said with a swagger when I pointed out to him that he whiffed a bit. I was right of course, and he managed to clear a two-yard space around himself every time he hit the small dancefloor. On top of that, he'd been on the Emu Bitter again and that had its usual effect on his bowels.

I did warn him, but he never listens.

Anyway, I'd somehow attracted the attention of this gorgeous girl in hot pants called Janet, and she was making it clear that she wanted more of me than was on display, if you know what I mean. A couple more pints of Swan for me and another rum and coke or two for her and our budding romance was starting to heat up nicely.

Unfortunately, things spiralled out of control when we decided to stagger outside, still kissing and hands wandering all over each other whilst locked in a passionate embrace. Not concentrating on where I was going, I crashed into the bouncer on the door. Well, I thought it was the bouncer, but it turned out to be Janet's dad, who'd come searching for his wayward daughter.

He was a big bloke was her dad, and so he was able to pick me up with one hand and pin me to the wall. Janet did mount a bit of a defence for me by jumping on his back and screaming, "Don't kill this one dad, we haven't done anything yet!" Clearly, I was just a pawn (or was it prawn...?) in her teenage rebellion.

Well, I think it was the 'yet' that did it, because her dad roared something that I couldn't decipher and threw me to the ground. By this time, quite a crowd had emerged from the pub, and some of the onlookers were taking bets on the likelihood of my survival.

Given the size of my attacker, the usually aggressive bouncer was looking a bit sheepish and keeping well out of the fray. Gary emerged to see what all the noise was about as he'd been in the dunny, and so he was a bit non-plussed to see me in the grip of the not-so-gentle giant.

"Isn't that your mate?" asked the bouncer, still looking the other way. "Never seen him before in my life," said my best pal. "Looks like a dickhead to me."

After the cops arrived and dragged the man mountain off me and sent him and Janet off with a warning, I was able to ascertain that my injuries were minor, well, in fact, I didn't seem to be hurt at all. I knew Swan Lager had magical qualities!

Once I'd regained my composure, I remonstrated with Gary for denying me in my hour of need. With a hurt expression on his face and a surprised tone in his voice, he responded with "I thought he meant the big bloke!"

Anyway, back to the situation in San Diego airport.

"I was confused by all the questions, and I panicked," was Gary's excuse as we finally left the airport as free men.

The whole matter had been cleared up when the test results came back from the lab. "Just a bag of Tide," laughed the US immigration official. Mum told me it was Omo, but I didn't argue with the man.

"Nevah argue whin ya's in frunt, mi bonny lad," my dad always said, and so I kept my mouth shut on the inaccuracy. Wise move, I think.

With no idea of how to get to Malibu, we caught a bus into town and headed for the first surf shop that we spotted. It turned out to be run by a nice, older guy who introduced himself as Truman. Well, Gary was fascinated with the coincidence—he'd come halfway around the world and found a possible relative. It took our new friend a good few minutes to explain that Truman was his first name. "What a strange name," puzzled my erstwhile bestie when the penny finally dropped.

Truman told us that he had a mate who was heading up to Malibu, and after a quick phone call, he managed to score us a lift with him.

Our driver was called Butch, a real nice guy, and he regaled us with local knowledge as we cruised up PCH (Pacific Coast Highway to those unfortunates amongst you that haven't been to So Cal), hugging the coast for over half of the three-hour drive.

We passed through Oceanside, San Clemente, Dana Point, San Onofre, Laguna, Newport Beach, Huntington Beach, and numerous other iconic Californian surf beaches—all the places that we'd read about in the magazines and always dreamed of visiting.

When we finally got to Malibu, Butch introduced us to his two housemates. A blonde-haired guy called Mike, and a Mexican-looking dude called Gerry.

It took only a few minutes for it to dawn on me. I thought he was familiar—Mike was no other than THE Mike. THE Mike Hynson who appeared in 'The Endless Summer'. I was talking to MIKE HYNSON! And Gerry was none other than GERRY LOPEZ, 'Mr Pipeline' himself! It was Gerry who quietly explained to us that our driver, Butch, was in fact Butch Van Artsdalen, who was one of the first people to surf Pipeline—years before Gerry made it his own.

We thought we'd died and gone to heaven!

After several cold beers, we seemed to be really hitting it off, and the guys said we could bunk down there for a few days. Score! Two young Aussies from Kelmscott staying with actual 'Living Legends'. It doesn't get much better than that!

We spent the next few days with the guys, surfing the Bu and Zuma Beach, and a string of other spots from Huntingdon Beach in the south up to Rincon and Santa Cruz in the north, depending on which break they judged would be firing.

"This is like something out of a movie," I said to Mike when we were sitting out the back near the point at Rincon, the 'Queen of the Coast'.

"Funny you should say that," he said. "Bruce is coming down in a few days to shoot some footage for his next movie."

"Whaaat!? THE legendary Bruce Brown who made 'The Endless Summer'?" I screeched.

"And he's bringing a couple of guys with him. Shaun Tomson and Nat," he added.

"Nat Young?" I squealed, unable to form proper words.

"Yep," Mike said casually. "He's Aussie too, you know."

Yeah, we knew!

So for the next few days me and GT were so excited that we hardly slept.

The day came around when the surfing royalty arrived, and we all piled into two trucks for the half-hour drive up to Rincon. I was sat next to Nat but couldn't seem to utter anything other than nervous schoolboy gibberish whenever he spoke to me.

Gerry was sitting in the front passenger seat, and he rescued me by asking about Western Australia, what the surf was like at our local breaks, and how they compared to Margaret River which, apparently, he'd heard of.

Such a nice, gentle-mannered guy. He said he was visiting Margaret River the following year as it was being considered for the fledgling professional circuit, and he asked if he could drop in and visit with me and GT. Can you imagine? Me bringing THE Gerry Lopez to Miami Bay in Falcon for a surf? Yahoo!

It was just on first light when we arrived at Rincon, and the guys had been right. A solid four-foot swell was pumping, with lines as far as the eye could see. Perfect!

We all helped Bruce carry his cameras and equipment down to the beach and then paddled out together.

Nat seemed to take a shine to my mate Gary and took him under his wing for the day, encouraging him to shred every inch of the waves and smash the lip with every hair-raising, crazy turn. GT decided he wanted to be called King Kong after that session which, he said, more befitted his new macho 'Animal' style.

I sat amongst Gerry, Mike, and Shaun. Such cool guys and all awesome surfers. I tried to copy Gerry's flowing and controlled style, picking the second or third wave in the set, reading the wave and responding to the ocean's movements rather than fighting them. 'Zen' Shaun called it. "Great theme for a book," I suggested. "The Zen of Surfing." Perhaps he'll write it one day.

My wave of the day was amazing—a clean five-foot beauty that was as smooth as glass.

I slid to my feet and really did feel 'at one' with the wave, gracefully carving the Mark of Zorro across its translucent face. A stall and then a few steps forward to hang ten for a good fifty yards of soul arch, before executing a perfect drop knee cut-back. The ride was almost a quarter of a mile long as I linked up section after section to finish at the beach in front of the highway.

Bruce waved me over to where he had set up the cameras and slapped me on the back. "Amazing wave, Ben. That will definitely be in the movie!"

Me, in a Bruce Brown movie? What did I say about dying and going to heaven?

Me and GT were completely whacked by the end of the day-long session, and it didn't take long for the hum of the engine and the rumble of PCH to send me off into a deep, surf-stoked sleep.

After what seemed like only a minute, I could hear GT's voice in my head screaming, "Wake up! Wake up, Ben, you drongo, answer the man!"

I lifted my head off the desk and tried to shake away the cobwebs, stretching and yawning as I did.

"Well?" said the immigration officer, how long will you be staying in the USA?"

A confused "Huh?" was all I could utter before it hit me.

Yep, you guessed it, I'd just been California Dreamin' again...!

The Pipeline

No matter how much I protested, Dad just wouldn't change his mind.

See, I was only a kid at the time and so didn't count, and he'd decided that we were going to spend six weeks in the UK. In Newcastle to be precise. He was from there originally and, well, I assumed he was homesick.

The rest of the family weren't too keen either, but Dad said that we needed to go to see my gran. Granddad, who I'd never met, had recently passed away, and so Dad wanted to comfort Gran and see her "Before it's too late," he said ominously. Too late for what, I wondered. Surely nothing could be that important!

After all, winter was here, and with it came the promise of consistent swells hitting the local spots in our beloved Miami Bay, Falcon.

Me and Gary had just finished repairing more dings on the Cordingley surfboard that we'd picked up at a garage sale. We still couldn't afford one each and so we had to share it, and we were surfing every day after school. I say surfing but, in reality, we spent most of our time arguing about how long each had had the board for. Or watching the more experienced surfers and trying to figure out how the heck they managed to look so stylish and make those awesome turns.

Still, with the help of Jim, an older guy who had been surfing there for years and who didn't hate us groms, we steadily improved.

Of course, we weren't allowed into the line-up with the rest of the local crew very often and, even then, they'd harass us just for fun. Part of the surfing rites of passage, I guess, but we hated it.

Most of it was harmless, but one guy in particular, Spit was his name, was just cruel and relentless. He was about sixteen and big for his age. He'd shout and scream if he caught us anywhere near him, and he would deliberately try to run us over if we were paddling out when he was on a wave. It didn't matter if we were doing the right thing by heading for the breaking section or paddling really wide; he was just a nasty piece of work.

And yes, he lived up to his nickname and would spit on you if he was close enough. Not just a bit of saliva but, you know, he'd empty his sinuses into his mouth and then let you have it.

Disgusting moron.

Nobody really liked him, but they sort of put up with him for his 'comedy' value, and the fact that he came in handy if there was ever any trouble with the odd group of Rockers that occasionally swung by the beach. Anyway, like all bullies, he finally picked on the wrong guy.

It turned out to be a kid called Bruce from Geraldton who was visiting his married sister in Mandurah. At fifteen, he was a few years older than us and, although scrawny and a bit awkward looking, he was already a really good surfer. He had cut his teeth on the powerful beach breaks around his hometown but had fallen in love with the points and reef breaks that we had in our neighbourhood.

Gary and I met him at Falcon one afternoon when there was a chest-high wave peeling left off the reef that we called 'Bitumens' and, to our amazement, there was no one else out. Bruce had this sort of confident style in the surf, and his smooth drop-knee turns were like something out of a surf movie.

Even his kick-out looked so casual and controlled. Me and Gary could still only barely manage to grab the board and then hang on for dear life as the waves broke over us at the end of their run to the beach.

Anyway, Gary had had about an hour on our Cordingley and so I called him to the beach to take my turn. He ended up with a nasty wipe-out by a sneaker set whilst he was, as usual, arguing the toss in an attempt to claim an extra few minutes on the board.

I did warn him, but he never listens.

After a couple of decent waves and a bit of story swapping with Bruce, I spotted him. Swaggering down the beach carrying his board, was our nemesis, Spit.

I paddled back over to Bruce and warned him that trouble was on the way and, as he was a stranger, he should probably make himself scarce. He looked over to Spit, who was now paddling towards us, smiled and said, "Nah, I'll be right, mate."

As I suspected, Spit made a beeline for the new face and was screaming threats before he'd got within twenty yards. "You're in my spot, you blow-in pisswit!" he snarled as he arrived alongside Bruce.

"Sorry, mate," said Bruce, "You've got it wrong. This is *my* spot just now and then it's Ben's turn."

Oh no, I thought, he must have a death wish!

Luckily, before Spit could unleash his fury on the challenger, Bruce paddled into the first wave of a nice set and took off on another stylish sixty-metre ride into the beach. Spit picked up the third wave in the set and arrived at the beach a moment later.

He was head and shoulders bigger than Bruce and, rushing in fast, he swung his signature knockout punch towards the poor little guy's head.

What none of us knew was that Bruce's dad was a semi-pro boxer who'd worked in a travelling circus and plied his craft in the Ring Tent. Despite his profession, he wasn't a violent man, but he had learned from experience that many others were, and so he'd made sure that all his three sons could look after themselves.

Bruce expertly ducked away from the jawbreaker, dummied with his left and, as Spit was leaning in after his swing at the little fella', our new-found friend launched his whole body forward and landed a powerful beauty with his right fist square on Spit's nose.

I heard the scream from where I was sitting, and Spit's nose exploded. He staggered backwards, covered in blood, and then, to everyone's surprise, he started to bawl his eyes out. Yep, as blood cascaded down his chest, the self-appointed, macho-man enforcer and hard case, Spit, was crying like a baby.

Whilst I'd been riveted by the action, I hadn't noticed that most of the local crew had arrived and had seen the unfolding drama from the lookout. They were now all hooting, laughing, and pointing at the blubbering bully.

We didn't see much of Spit after that. We figured he'd found somewhere else to surf and another set of groms to intimidate, who maybe hadn't heard the story. I'd like to think that he'd learned his lesson but, anyway, at least he didn't bother us anymore. Without Spit, the vibe at all the local breaks became much more friendly and laid back. Strange how 'one bad apple can spoil the barrel' as my mum used to say.

Anyway, back to my dad.

"Yaz cumin' whether ya likes it or yaz duzzn't," he roared. "And no, yaz not stayin' with ya bluddy mate Gary—weez all goin' tigether an' that's the end of it!"

Two days later, dressed in our Sunday best, we boarded the Boeing 707 at the airport in Perth and started the long trek to somewhere that I didn't know, and that I didn't want to know.

The plane was huge, and it looked brand new—just like a shiny, silver bird, and the take-off with those jet engines was awesome. Mum didn't seem to think so though, as she had to grab a sick bag from the seat pocket and proceeded to fill it with the eggs and bacon that we'd all had for breakfast earlier.

After about five hours, we landed in Jakarta, and this was followed by stops in Colombo, Karachi, Tehran, and Munich, all to refuel, I suppose. Mum managed to fill a sick bag every time we took off, even though she'd eaten none of the great food that we were served on those posh trays by the smiling stewardess. Strange that, and so by the time we finally landed in London, she wasn't fairing too well.

As ever though, she kept her tribe in check and marshalled us onto various trains and buses for the rest of the day, until we arrived in Dad's hometown of Newcastle-Upon-Tyne.

"Wye aye, it's graate ta be back!" exclaimed Dad as we staggered into Gran's tiny, terraced house at number thirty-one Johnson Street.

It had a small lounge room that Gran called the 'Front Room', and an even smaller kitchen with a gas cooker, a tall cupboard that had a drop-down shelf that acted as a bench-top, a small table with a blue plastic cover, and a sink under the window. The back door led out onto a small, paved backyard with an outside dunny.

Upstairs were two bedrooms, one occupied by Gran, and the other was spare and had two single beds, and there was no bathroom. This was going to be cosy!

It was the beginning of August, but the sunless sky was dark grey and seemed to touch the tops of the light poles that lined the street on both sides. A steady drizzle blew in waves across the cobbled paving stones and the grey slate roofs. Everything was grey, even Gran's cat.

Gran was a tiny woman with a permanent smile on her face and bright red, rosy cheeks that made her look constantly embarrassed. Her thin, grey hair and the lines on her brow and cheeks spoke of years of hard work and worry and, looking around the tiny, modest home, I wondered if it had all been worth it. She was a lovely lady who was generous with her hugs, and she seemed to be able to put my dad in his place with just a sideways glance. A joy to behold!

We settled in, and me and my brother Gerry were allocated the sofa and so had to sleep head to toe. This made for a few sibling scraps as his feet smelled like rotting fish and were about an inch from my nose. He was bigger than me and so usually won the altercations and, to avoid further conflict, I started going to sleep with one of Gran's scarves wrapped over my nose and mouth. It wasn't a cure, but it at least improved things.

We'd been there about two days when the paperboy delivered a weekly Trading Post-style rag called 'Exchange and Mart', a hangover from Granddad, I guess. Bored and with nothing else to do, I slowly browsed through it, and, buried deep in the sports section, I stumbled across an advert titled *'Surfboard Plans'*. Excitedly, I read on. *'Build your own surfboard with our easy-to-follow instructions. Only Ten Shillings'*.

What? A surfboard for ten bob? Well, for the plans at least, and so after a full day of pleading with Mum, she agreed that I could spend some of my holiday money on the plans. I carefully crafted a letter and a large, return-addressed envelope, and then sped off to the post office to buy a postal order and send it to somewhere called Devon.

I could hardly contain myself for the next week as I waited each day for the postman to arrive with my precious cargo. Finally, just about a week and a half after I'd sent off my money, the large brown self-addressed envelope dropped through the post slot in the front door.

I carefully removed the tightly folded plans and then opened them on the floor of the front room, almost filling it. The huge sheet was just over eight feet by three feet and was marked with a full-scale drawing showing the outline and dimensions of the board. The other side had the large nose block and tail block, along with the square rails, the three ribs, and an outline of the skeg. Separate from the plan was another sheet showing the promised 'simple' instructions to build the hollow, plywood board. Simple? A Chinese puzzle, more like!

The next week was spent assembling the materials which included an eight-foot by four-foot sheet of three-sixteenths inch marine ply, glue, fixings, lengths of half inch pine for the side rails, solid two-inch pine for the nose and tail blocks, and three-eighths inch ply for the ribs and skeg. And, of course, a tin of marine varnish to finish it off. Thankfully, Gran chipped in to help me buy everything, which basically cleared me out of my spending money.

I worked out that the idea was to trace the outline of the deck and bottom and the other components directly from the plans onto the plywood and other materials. With this achieved and using the rudimentary tools from Granddad's toolbox, I set about crafting my masterpiece in the tiny backyard. Luckily, the rain had moved on to another part of the 'Green and Pleasant Land' and, now and again, the sun even peeked out in between the clouds.

My gran had a transistor radio that I set up near the open back door, and so I was able to listen to Radio Caroline, an amazing pirate radio station that had cool DJs broadcasting from somewhere in the North Sea. It was the only one worth listening to, and it played all the songs from the UK and US Hit Parades.

By the end of the week I'd learned all the words of the Top Ten hits and loudly sang along to the likes of The Animals; The Beatles; Dave Dee, Dozy, Beaky, Mick, and Tich (yep, there was really a band called that!); Chris Montez; The Rolling Stones; The Kinks; and The Beach Boys. Their 'Help Me Rhonda' was one of my favourites and I'd belt it out the chorus at the top of my voice.

That usually brought a torrent of complaints from inside the house along with threats to take away the trannie, as everyone else sat in the gloom watching the telly all day.

Strange family I've got.

Day by day, I filled the backyard with sawdust, wood shavings and offcuts as the board took shape. Carpentry skills weren't my strong point and so, as hard as I tried, my creation didn't quite look like the illustration enclosed with the plans. The square rails weren't exactly the right shape for the intended rocker, and the outline had gone astray on the deck towards the tail—the result of a slip with the handsaw. I couldn't afford another sheet of ply, and so I had to adjust the bottom to match, putting an interesting kink in the finished shape. I comforted myself with the fact that it was, at least, completely unique.

Despite this, and a few other errors which further taxed my skills and my nerves, I'd done it; I'd actually managed to build my own surfboard!

I carefully wrote 'Ben' on the nose in big letters with a thick marker pen, and then lovingly applied three coats of marine varnish, allowing the requisite light sanding and twenty-four-hour wait between applications. I stood back to admire my creation and, up until then, it was probably the proudest day of my life.

Mum, Dad, and my brother Gerry didn't seem to get it though. Gerry just shrugged his shoulders and shook his head. Mum smiled and patted me on my head, whilst Dad could only say, "And what the bluddy hell are yaz going to do with that thing ya daft puddin' head?" What is this fixation they've got with my head?

It was only Gran that could see the beauty of my labour of love. With an excited smile and clapping her hands, she gave me one of her signature hugs.

"Wye aye Benny, I think it's proper nice pet, proper nice. Yeh've done a grand job of it, so yeh have," she beamed.

Thanks, Gran.

Now the next challenge was to see how Nautilus, as I called my trusty new steed, would do in the surf.

As it turned out, opportunity knocked the following weekend when my Uncle Ernie and Aunty Meg, both of whom seemed to know me even though I had no idea who they were, invited us to join them on a trip to Blackpool, wherever that was. He said it was 'the seaside' and so I assumed it must have a beach and, therefore, surf. "Let's go then!" I screamed inside, whilst maintaining a polite be-seen-but-not-heard demeanour on the outside.

Saturday came and, after wrapping Nautilus in a woollen blanket and strapping it to the roof, we all piled into Uncle Ernie's huge, black Humber Snipe station wagon, or estate car as he called it, and headed off for the coast. Well, as it turned out, it was the very distant coast, as Blackpool was nearly two hundred miles away—even though there was a beach resort called Whitley Bay that was only ten miles up the road. Strange choice, Uncle Ernie, I mused, and I hope Blackpool is worth it!

Five hours later, and after my brother Gerry won a shilling

for the apparently traditional pommie contest to be the first to spot Blackpool Tower in the far distance, we checked into Mrs Benfold's guest house on York Road. It was about three quarters of a mile north of Blackpool Tower, which Mum said was a replica of the Eiffel Tower in Paris. Fancy town was Blackpool.

Luckily, it was only a few minutes' walk to the beach and so, as soon as I could, I got into my boardies, grabbed my board, and headed for the water. There was a monument on the beachfront at the end of the street, and so I headed for that and thought that I could use it as my line-up marker.

Well, first of all, I should mention that my glistening new, hand-crafted beauty, Nautilus, weighed a ton, and so I perched it on my head and staggered down the street. It was tough going, and I swear that I was two inches shorter by the time I got to the beach!

Secondly, when I got to the seafront, I had to descend about thirty stone steps to get onto the strangely empty beach itself, as a huge sea wall ran in both directions for as far as the eye could see. The water was also a fair way in the distance because of the massive low tide which, I later found out, was common for Blackpool's very flat beach. I trudged across the empty sand, dragging my board, for what seemed like ages before I finally got to the surf.

And thirdly, calling it surf is a massive exaggeration, as the murky, brown water—even the foam on breaking waves was a frothy, matching colour—showed no real signs of any swell but was being pushed into a wind-blown slop by a stiff onshore wind.

Undeterred, I pushed my board through the shore break, hopped on, and knee-paddled to where I thought there might be a peak. Nearly an hour later, I was still looking for the aforementioned peak to show itself and was just about to give up when, driven by the increasing wind, a sloppy chest-high wave appeared.

I paddled for my life, and my heavy steed finally started to move down the face of the brown breaker. I slid to my feet and angled my board left to take advantage of the only bit of the wave face that looked surfable.

Nautilus did me proud and locked into the bumpy face, as best its square rails would allow. As I picked up speed, I managed to put in a couple of decent bottom turns and then, after a few more seconds in trim, I kicked out and paddled back to the take-off spot where I'd been sitting. My new, hand-crafted hollow-ply surfboard had passed its first test with flying colours!

I got two more waves and, on the second one, which was shoulder-high and surprisingly nice given the horrible conditions, Nautilus came into his own. I picked up the wave after only two double-arm paddles and my pride and joy flew down the steep face at what seemed like Mach two. A stylish cut-back set me up for a ten-second trim before I was flipped off by the crashing honey-coloured monster.

I hung onto Nautilus for dear life as the surprisingly powerful force tumbled me over a few times. It was difficult to see through the squalls that now blew stronger, and so, after a couple more failed attempts and another half an hour of waiting in the cold, biting wind, I decided to give up and paddle in.

What seemed like a near hurricane was whipping the water's surface into an angry mess, and I struggled to get the now even heavier board moving. My arms were like spaghetti and my lungs screaming for respite by the time I neared the place that I'd come onto the beach.

Unbeknown to me, and whilst I was distracted with my board's maiden voyage, the tide had filled in at an alarming rate, and there was no longer any beach. The waves were now crashing halfway up the fifteen-foot sea wall and, to my surprise, quite a crowd had gathered to watch my antics.

Standing at the top of the steps, there was a lifeguard-cum-beach-inspector and a policeman, resplendent in his bobby's helmet and wearing a cape against the storm. Both were screaming something at me, but I couldn't hear them over the roaring wind and crashing waves.

It was pretty tricky getting to the base of the steps and a couple of times I got thrown against the sea wall. The lifeguard came down the slippery, stone staircase as far as he could without ending up in the drink himself. He grabbed my arm and pulled me and my board to safety. I had to remove the cork deck-plug and drain almost a gallon of the brown stuff from my board before I could lift it and stagger up to street level.

The policeman continued to scream at me.

"You bloody idiot! What were you doing? You could have drowned or, or, or even worse!" he bellowed over the applause from the crowd, who were now surrounding us and slapping me on the back, apparently glad to see me alive.

A passing tram stopped, the driver probably assuming that there was a drowning or, perhaps, something equally interesting in progress that he didn't want to miss. His passengers also poured off their green and white carriage to join the melee, swelling the crowd to a reasonable turn-out at a Kenwick Footy Club home game.

"Owoo, Arthur," said one lady to her husband, both dressed in plastic raincoats against the now pelting rain, "Hay speeks reet funny, dun't hay? Mustn't bee frum round heer…"

"Prob'ly a bluddy Yank," said hubby disdainfully, perhaps still remembering the thousands of American troops that flooded the country during the war and swept the English girls off their feet whilst their men were elsewhere.

Not used to such attention, I was enjoying the celebrity status, and a loud cheer went up when, grinning, I gave them all a wave to reassure everyone that their hero was fine. I thought they might raise me on their shoulders and transport me home but, alas, PC Plod had other ideas.

"And where is the paddle for that, that canoe contraption?" he said angrily, pointing at my now rather forlorn-looking board. "Give me your name and address, your parents will hear about this!" he spat whilst brandishing his notebook. Once he knew I was just visiting and that the guesthouse was close by, he unceremoniously dragged me away from the crowd of well-wishers and back to Mrs Benfold's.

Needless to say, Dad wasn't happy and Mum had to get between us before he throttled me.

Uncle Ernie was more interested in the state of my now somewhat battered board and wanted to hear all the details of my marine adventure. He almost wet himself laughing when I told him exactly where I'd surfed and asked him why the sea was so murky and brown.

In between gasps for air, he explained. "It's one of the sewer outlets, you dope! They pump it from Blackpool Sewage Works, and it ends up a couple of hundred yards out in the sea, right in line with the monument. "Didn't ya see the big pipe, ya daft head?" he added. There goes my head again!

No, I didn't notice the pipe, but I *was* feeling a bit queasy to be honest, and it would be some time before the brown tinge finally disappeared from my boardies.

But never mind all that because I'm pretty sure that, on that wet and windswept day in August 1966, I was the first person (and perhaps the last...) to ever surf at Blackpool, Lancashire, England. That, of course, gave me naming rights for the surf break and so, after some thought, I settled on 'Cess Pits'.

Fitting don't you think? Particularly when they're pumping out through The Pipeline!

The Sandals

"Be quiet under there you two!" hissed Sue in a half shout, half whisper, "It's not funny, the manager is at the door!"

You see, me and Gary were hiding under the bed and giggling like schoolboys in Sue and Tania's room at the Dunsborough Beach Hotel. This hiding spot was a strange place I know, but it was all we could think of in a moment of panic.

Our new surfing mate, Chaz, was spending the weekend with a gorgeous girl called Marjorie who he'd met in Fremantle, and so me and Gary had taken Friday off work and headed down to Yallingup late on Thursday arvo. This meant that we could have three full days surfing our favourite spots, and we'd heard that the weekend was lining up for light offshores and a decent three to four-foot swell—just right!

Of course, everyone else in Perth had had the same idea,

and so the caravan parks at the beach and near the pub were chockers. Not enough space to lay out our swags, never mind pitch the tent that Gary had brought along. Unusual for Gary to think of our comfort; we were usually happy to sleep in the van or on the beach. However, the rangers in the area were pretty active for some reason and not very friendly, and so we decided that a few beers would help us come up with some ideas of where we could rest our heads.

We headed for the Yallingup Hotel, the only local hostelry in Yalls, but found the beer garden deserted and the hotel shut up tight.

We found out why later that evening when we bumped into Dave, the hotel's glassie. The unscheduled and, for us, extremely inconvenient closure was caused by a clearly incompetent and negligent (and probably half-pissed) employee who left a water tap running and in full flow after closing time.

Apparently, the scoundrel was, shall we say, distracted whilst engaging in a passionate triste with another staff member on one of the pool tables. Unaware of the unfolding disaster at ground level, still naked and after the customary cigarette, they fell fast asleep in a lovers' embrace.

As the first light of dawn filtered through the stained glass windows, the happy couple were awoken by a strange gurgling sound. Stretching and yawning, they hopped off their love nest only to discover that they were knee-deep in cold water and the bar, hotel reception, and posh dining room were all now under a good foot or two of H_2O.

The notice on the hotel door said that it would be some time before the venue would be reopening, and we were left to ponder whether the errant employees would still be part of the workforce. Maybe not.

So, with the prospect of a dry weekend, we had to find another watering hole.

Our choices were to drive to Margaret River, which was a good hour away and could be tricky in the dark, or head to Dunsborough, which was only fifteen minutes away and had a choice of drinking venues. Our favourite spot in town was the Dunsborough Arms, which served ice-cold Swan Lager and usually had skimpies serving in the main bar on the weekends. They also had live bands and a great DJ spinning the decks from Thursday through to Saturday.

Swan Lager, skimpies, bands, and a DJ? No brainer!

The pub was packed to the rafters, and a band was banging out some good rocking tunes, and so we settled in for a few beers and grabbed some hot tucker to fill our empty stomachs. When we'd finished the food and the beer had loosened our legs, we joined the crowd on the dancefloor to strut some moves.

Gary, as usual, was throwing himself around in an attempt to attract the attention of a girl or two. Instead, he almost knocked a tray full of glasses out of the hand of a waitress and only succeeded in attracting the attention of the nearest bouncer.

I did warn him, but he never listens.

Luckily, the bouncer was called Gavin, and he knew Gary's sister and so he let my bestie off with a whispered warning. Whatever he said certainly worked because Gazza settled down and was even quite stylish, dancing to next couple of songs. This caught the eye of a girl called Tania who was stunning in the looks department. She was already quite tipsy and couldn't seem to keep her hands off old Gary, and I must admit that I was feeling quite jealous.

They danced steamily with their bodies glued to each other as the DJ took over for the final session and slowed things down a bit and by this time, they were in danger of getting themselves thrown out for lewd behaviour. Not surprisingly, their passionate groping didn't seem to please the guy that Tania had been dancing with for most of the night before old Gazza stole her heart. Pushing his way across the dancefloor, her jilted would-be lover headed straight for my mate.

Discretion being the better part of valour, I took a couple of steps backwards as the potential pugilist, who resembled a large and very angry bear, loomed ever closer. I knew Gary could look after himself, but the other guy looked pretty big and pretty upset, and so I thought some space might be prudent. You know, where I could step in if needed, or make a run for it if things turned ugly.

He rushed towards Gary, pointing menacingly and mouthing some pretty choice phrases about what he was going to do to him. Shocked by the impending catastrophe, Gary was galvanized into one of his last-ditch 'avoidance' moves.

You see, my mate is a peace-loving and soulful guy, and by no means aggressive. He'd often just walk away (or more likely run!) from some numbnut looking for trouble, even though, behind that dopey smile, he could be quite a tough cookie when he wanted to be. He would usually do anything to avoid a fight, and I'd seen him do things like this before, usually when he was cornered and needed to get out of trouble fast.

As the guy charged in, Gary swiftly uncoupled himself from Tania, threw his arms in the air and pretended to faint, hopefully stumbling away from danger. His would-be attacker didn't react quickly enough to the shifting target and managed to trip over Gary's outstretched leg. He went head over heels and finished up spread-eagled on the dancefloor. Sensing his ploy had worked in an unexpected way, Gary regained his balance and shouted, "He's pissed!" over the screams of dancers that Mr Grizzly had almost floored during his dive.

This brought the bouncers in fast, and, despite his noisy protests, they dragged the struggling ruffian out into the street and had a quiet word with him, in the inimitable way that bouncers did back then.

"Geez mate, that was awesome!" I shouted over the music, genuinely impressed. "Poor bloke tripped up," grinned Gary.

Tania, now even more in love with her hero, took us over to the bar and introduced me to her friend, Sue. She was about five-foot six, with long and flowing auburn hair, a cute turned-up nose and she was dressed in a trendy, low cut, maxi dress. I was smitten! The four of us danced and drank and danced some more.

Sue was proving to be really hot on the dancefloor and, as things slowed down even further, she squeezed me in so tight that I thought I was going to burst—in more ways than one!

Last orders were called, the DJ played his last ballad, and after one more smooch on the dancefloor, we spilled out onto the street laughing and singing. We found a quiet spot in a shop doorway for a bit more kissing and groping but, just when things were really heating up between me and Sue, we were moved on by a passing police patrol. Just my luck.

With nowhere else to go, and after a quick whispered conference out of our earshot, the girls suggested that we should all go back to their place to continue the party.

We crept across the hotel car park and stealthily slipped into their room. Things were looking up!

The bedroom was small and sparsely furnished, with yellow painted brick walls. It had a double bed covered in a fluffy, purple bedspread which sported a large, suspicious stain along with a couple of cigarette burns in the middle. There was a tiny, tired looking bathroom in the corner which smelled decidedly suspect and the carpet had definitely seen better days. But, hey, it hands down beat sleeping in the van and dodging the ranger now, didn't it?

We'd picked up a six-pack before we left the pub, and Gary

passed a beer to each of us as we sat on the bed and chatted.

GT and Tania were soon moving up a gear, groaning and pashing noisily in between drinks. Me and Sue were doing nicely too, although given the way that she'd been looking at Gary on the way back from the pub, I think she might have felt that she had drawn the short straw. Really? "My animal attraction, mate," Gary would often say when he managed to woo a real babe. "They like a bit of rough sometimes, Ben old son, and I'm happy to oblige," he'd quip with a superior look on his face. Maybe he was right. I'll never know the answer though because I'm, you know, handsome, debonair and cool. Well, that's my argument anyway!

Just when things were really warming up again with me and Sue, there was an almighty banging at the door.

"Who've you got in there!? I can hear them, you know!" shouted an angry male voice. "Don't think I don't know what you're up to! This is a respectable place, and I'll have none of that hippy, free-love malarkey here!" he screamed.

Free love? What planet was he from? Perhaps he could tell us where to find it!

Apparently, it was Mr Rhodes, the hotel manager, and he must have seen us creeping across the car park. Well, he probably heard us because, as we all know, trying to be quiet when you're drunk is not that easy.

With seconds to spare before the killjoy carried out his threat to use his passkey to get in, me and Gary dived under the bed and lay as still as we could, trying not to giggle too much or even breathe too loud. The girls continued to protest their innocence through the locked door, but, undeterred, our accuser continued his tirade. Sue knelt on the floor and put her finger to her lips, signalling to us to be dead silent, and then she adjusted her dress and straightened her hair before opening the door.

The fuming manager burst in and rushed around the room like a madman, scanning every corner with a crazed look in his eyes. Intent on uncovering the carnal plot, he then threw open the bathroom door, figuring it was probably the most likely hiding place for the sex-crazed suspects. He found it empty except, that is, for Tania who, with knickers around her ankles, was sitting on the toilet pretending to take a pee. She screamed at the now retreating intruder as he quickly reversed back into the bedroom, mumbling an apology.

He shook off the embarrassing incident and tiptoed over to the wardrobe and swung open the doors with a flourish, like a magician's reveal in a disappearing act. Finding it similarly empty, except for the girls' clothes, he spun around and surveyed the rest of the room, wheezing as he breathed heavily in frustration.

"I know you're here somewhere!" he grumbled angrily, sounding increasingly disappointed that perhaps he was wrong, and that maybe the Woodstock Festival had, indeed, passed Dunsborough by.

Tania had emerged from the bathroom and was now shouting at him, telling him he was a pervert bursting in on her ablutions and insisted that he should get out.

Flustered, he cast his eyes around the room one more time and, still seething, he went to leave.

Just at that critical moment, Gary, unable to hold it any longer, let out one of his signature belches. On the right day, and with the right combination of food and beer in his stomach, my mate Gazza could shatter a wine glass when he let rip. So there was no chance that it could have gone unnoticed, unless, of course, Mr Manager was deaf.

"I knew it!" he screamed as he threw back the overhanging bedspread and thrust his head downwards to view his prey. This was to prove to be a big mistake, as Gary's belches were not only loud but also pungent. His intestines have always been a bit of an enigma, but suffice it to say that the smells that emerged from both ends of Gary's digestive tract were powerful enough to strip paint.

I'd built up a measure of immunity over the years but, alas, our erstwhile pursuer had no such preparation for the olfactory onslaught. His head recoiled from the sudden impact of the escaping stench on his sinuses and, eyes now streaming, he banged his noggin hard on the bed's iron frame.

Dazed, he slumped backwards and, rubbing the crown of his shiny, bald head, he sat groaning on the floor. An egg-shaped lump was already swelling up quite nicely as he continued to whimper in pain.

This gave me and Gazza the seconds that we needed to extricate ourselves from our hiding place and leg it through the open door. Our potential captor was determined not to be denied his quarry though, and made a grab for Gary as he made his run for freedom. From his position on the dusty carpet, the not-so-friendly manager couldn't quite get a good grip on the human whippet and only succeeded in seizing Gary's foot. This temporarily halted his escape, but a quick flick of his leg and the hapless captor was left holding a sweaty sandal.

"Sorry you lost your shoe, mate," I said breathlessly to Gary when we finally reached the safe haven of the van.

"That's OK, Ben, it wasn't mine, it was yours. I borrowed them from your bag when we were getting ready. I didn't think you'd mind," he added with a hurt expression on his face.

"What? They were my favourite Huaraches, you lemon! I bought them on our trip to So Cal, for Heaven's sake," I said, banging my hand on the side of the van. "I thought they looked bloody familiar!"

"Sorry, Ben," he said sheepishly whilst offering me the now pungent single piece of footwear that had survived the drama. "No thanks, mate, you can keep it," I snapped whilst recoiling from the stench.

"One's not much use to me," mumbled Gary, and with a dismissive shrug of his shoulders, he tossed my memory-filled and precious footwear into a nearby bin.

We never did see Tania and Sue again, but we did hear from Gavin the bouncer that, in the end, they managed to appease their landlord. After being reminded of his untimely and uninvited entry into the girls' bathroom, he decided to avoid any further trouble and withdrew his eviction notice. Our consciences were therefore clear.

Me and Gary spent an uncomfortable night in the van parked in a side street only to be awoken at an unseemly hour by the garbage collection truck on its rounds. Feeling pretty seedy, we headed off to get ourselves the well-known local hangover cure—a breakfast pie and coffee from the bakery in the main street.

A short drive to Yallingup and we snagged a spot in the near- empty car park overlooking Main Break. Strange, we thought, as it was usually packed by six thirty. This was our preferred spot to park as we could scramble down the rocks, paddle over the reef and through the keyhole, and straight out to the take-off spot.

Not today, though. We struggled to keep our feet against the roaring onshore wind that had whipped our beloved break into a giant washing machine. So much for the forecast!

We knew that Smiths Beach and Indijup would also be blown out, but there was a slim chance that PKs or The Farm might be working and protected from the howler. So we headed north only to find that the swell wasn't wrapping around into these more protected spots. The weather report on the radio was for more of the same for the rest of the weekend and so, dejected and rapidly running out of ideas, we decided to pull the pin on our Yallingup weekend and head back nearer to our home breaks, in the hope that the poor weather hadn't yet reached there.

The radio was blasting and me and Gary were singing

along at the top of our voices and, after a couple of hours driving, we let some air out of the tyres on my trusty panel van and headed off the highway and down the sand track towards the usually reliable break at Tim's Thicket. We shouldn't have bothered as the onshore blow started rocking the van as soon as we emerged from the protection of the sand dunes and reached the beach.

Melros and Dixieland were both the same and so, dejected, we decided to head to the Miami Deli to fill our now grumbling stomachs.

As we hit the carpark, we realised that we must have been suffering from brain-block or something, because we could have saved a lot of time and just headed straight back to Falcon.

The beach directly in front of the deli, known as Miami Bay, faces northwest and has high dunes protecting it from the south westerlies. On the right day, the point produces waist to chest-high peelers that run for sixty or seventy metres to the soft sand beach. Awesome!

Today was no exception, and we stood there open-mouthed, unable to speak as we surveyed the glassy and empty waves. What were we thinking, dammit? We'd wasted most of the day hunting around in the wind when we could have been surfing one of our favourite breaks!

We scrambled out of the van with our boards and paddled out to the take-off spot. Gary was first up on a nice slider that had some punch, and he was able to milk it all the way and literally step off onto the beach. I followed him on the next wave in the set and ran off the front of my board in the shore break.

Two hours later and a bucket full of waves under our belts, we succumbed to the hunger pangs and paddled in. We headed to the deli, and both tucked into a freshly baked pie followed by a milkshake. Perfect post-surf tucker!

Suitably replenished, we sat on the foreshore and watched the sun set over the dunes.

"Y'know, Ben," said Gary. "This has been a crackin' session. I think we should have definitely stayed home this weekend."

"But you wouldn't have met Tania then," I said reassuringly.

Nodding and with a reflective look on his face, Gary responded. "Yeah, you're right mate, she was hot, really hot, but at least if we'd stayed here, you'd still have The Sandals."

Blame it on the Boogie

It started as an awesome day out with our new buddy, Tom, but sadly, it didn't end that way.

You see, me and Gary had arrived in San Diego and, after a short but stressful delay in immigration, we tried to get to Malibu but, unfortunately, we didn't make it. It wasn't anybody's fault, but Gary did make the point that, "If we'd bought that map in the airport then none of this would have ever happened!"

Thanks, Gazza, but I'm not so sure.

Anyway, our journey to 'The Bu' got off to a good start at the airport where we managed to hitch a ride with a nice Mexican family. They didn't speak any English, and our Spanish was non-existent, but we got by with a bit of charades and lots of hand signals.

We mimed some surfing moves and repeated "Malibu",

"Malibu" a few times, and they seemed to get it—if their nodding heads, thumbs up, and wide grins were anything to go by that is. So off we set on our three-hour journey up Pacific Coast Highway 101, or PCH as it is known to us cool dudes.

I must admit that I was a bit puzzled when we started climbing those mountains, but at least we could see the ocean in the distance. The far, far distance.

We were both beat, and Gary was fast asleep by this stage, and I soon drifted off too. I woke about an hour and a half later just as we passed a sign for the Mojave Desert. At this point, I was beginning to wonder, but our driver just grinned again and reassured me by nodding his head enthusiastically when I queried his navigation skills and repeated, "Malibu? Malibu?"

So, a few hours later, we arrived in Las Vegas.

Our Mexican friends dropped us off in front of the Malibu Inn, a tiny motel a couple of miles south of the main Vegas strip. Lots more grins and handshakes later, the Mexicans turned the car around and, waving out of the windows, they headed off down the highway to who knows where.

We didn't see them again, but we resolved there and then to learn some Spanish for our future adventures.

In case you don't know, Las Vegas is in the landlocked state of Nevada and exactly three-hundred and twelve miles due east of Malibu. It is also just under five hours non-stop driving from San Diego airport, and it doesn't have any surf or, for that matter, a beach.

We stood in the motel car park gazing at the less than salubrious property. It was hot enough to melt the bitumen, and there was a constant scorching breeze that dried your eyes if you were daft enough to spend too much time outside.

What the ...?

We'd had problems with our travels before but thankfully, much closer to home. Like the time we were driving my panel van across the Nullarbor on the first leg of the journey that would be our 'East Coast Surfari'.

For those of you who don't know, the Nullarbor Plain is harsh and barren desert country that stretches almost a thousand miles between Norseman in Western Australia (which is around seven hours driving east of Perth) and Ceduna in South Australia. The Eyre Highway crosses this vast expanse of nothing, is very straight, and covers a big chunk of the distance between Perth and Adelaide.

Forty degrees mid-day temperatures and no air-con in the van meant that by the time we'd covered the two hundred and fifty miles from Perth to Southern Cross, we were toasted. We decided that it might be a good idea to do most of the future driving at night.

So, the next day, we laid up and slept in the shade of the van until dusk before heading off east again. We drove for the three or four hours to Norseman and onto the Eyre Highway, and all was going well until, that is, we met the kangaroo.

Out of the darkness appeared this huge red male; his

eyes lit up like beacons in my headlights. He was just standing there in the middle of the road, all six foot of him. I slammed on the brakes and swerved, missing him by inches, and careered off the side of the bitumen.

The van flipped onto its roof and then upright again before skidding into the scrub. It happened so fast that we hardly moved in our seats. We ended up in a ditch and needed a few moments to collect ourselves and to stop screaming.

Gary was the worst. He was bellowing, "PLEASE GOD DELIVER US!" "PLEASE GOD DELIVER US!" over and over. This was the first time I'd ever seen his religious side. Very interesting, I thought.

As for me, I was just screaming.

Once we'd calmed down, we climbed out and inspected my trusty steed. In the darkness there didn't seem to be a scratch on her but, given that we were both shaking like leaves, we decided it might be a good idea to wait until dawn before carrying on our journey in daylight—metal sweat box or not.

After we'd got used to the dingos howling and calmed ourselves sufficiently from the accident, we shifted our boards and slept soundly in the back of the van.

We awoke to the sound of a road train passing just a few yards from our tin bedroom, and the backdraft from the huge truck rocked the van so violently that we thought it might flip us over again.

When we'd composed ourselves, we crawled out into the cool morning sunlight and lit a fire to warm up some beans and make a cup of tea. As the temperature hit thirty-five degrees within an hour or so, we realised that maybe we should have got some miles on the clock before stopping for vittels.

Pretty soon we could have cooked eggs on the bonnet of the van to go with our beans, and so we got moving again, but this time in broad, albeit stinking hot, daylight.

We drove all day without having to dodge any other roos, or cattle, emus and wild goats, all of which regularly wandered perilously close to the highway but, thankfully, stayed out of our way.

After a good roasting in the incessant heat of our mobile oven, we arrived at Cocklebiddy Roadhouse, a typical remote Outback hostelry, just as the light was fading. We filled the van up with petrol and then hit the diner to fill ourselves up with burger and chips, rounded off with a couple of jugs of icy cold beer.

That's when we spotted them.

Two gorgeous girls dressed only in shorts and bikini tops, and looking half dead, walked into the roadhouse begging for water. Well, being gentlemen and all, we ushered them to our booth, and they proceeded to pour a full jug of beer down their throats. We could see they were grateful because they kept smiling in between gulps and, once they were rehydrated on 'Four X' (no Swan Lager here unfortunately), they filled us in on their plight.

Apparently, their car had run out of fuel about five miles back up the highway, and they'd walked here. They said that they hadn't seen another vehicle in the two hours it had taken them to hike along the highway, and so they were exhausted. They needed a lift back with some fuel and, of course, we said we'd oblige but that it would have to wait until the morning light. After all, it was getting late, and we were the wrong side of a few jugs by then.

So, introductions done, a few more beers and some music on the jukebox, things were going pretty well with Brenda and Louise. It was clear that Brenda and Gary were getting on a storm. You see, Gary has always had a penchant for big boobs, well, it borders on an obsession really, and his new love interest was extremely well blessed in that department. So, Gary was in full flight with his best chat up lines to accompany his dancing to the available disco numbers. He was really into the disco music scene at that time and was strutting his best moves.

Me and Louise weren't doing too badly either, and we soon slipped outside so that we could pash in the relative privacy of the now almost deserted fuel station. She had her tongue so far down my throat that I was almost gagging, and her wandering hands were definitely raising the stakes for the rest of the night, if you know what I mean!

After my previous missed opportunities in that department, I was trying to keep calm and take it slowly, but that was proving hard to do.

Giggling, Louise led me to the back of the van and pinned

me against the rear doors whilst Brenda and Gary joined us outside. They were soon on the bonnet and, it seemed, determined to give the front suspension a workout.

Louise's hands were all over me and then inside my jeans, and then just as I was about to make my move—not sure what that might have been but, as a keen amateur, I was about to do something—the girls seemed to instantly sober up and bade us both good night.

They claimed the back of the van for their boudoir, leaving me and Gary, shall we say, very hot under the collar and searching for somewhere to sleep.

They pulled out our boards and bags so they could stretch out, and we decided to cool our ardour with another beer or two in the bar.

"Maybe tomorrow," said Gary. "They are *so* worth the wait, and I think Brenda could be 'the one'," he added in an unexpected show of emotion. Strange, I thought, for my normally committed-bachelor buddy.

Anyway, I nodded and took another gulp of Four X whilst crossing my fingers and toes.

It had been a long day and so we slept soundly under the veranda at the back of the outdoor dunnies, which was fairly handy given the beer we'd consumed. Waking early to the sweet sound of grunting followed by flushing, and the not-so-sweet smells, we stuck our heads under the cold tap to shake off the cobwebs. We casually sauntered around to the car park to wake the girls and offer them a cup of tea and, hopefully, a kiss or two and who knows what else!

It was a bit of a surprise to find that our newfound potential lovers and the van were nowhere to be seen. Yes, you've guessed it, she'd lifted the keys out of my jeans pocket during all that pashing and groping. They looked such nice girls and, well, I wasn't expecting this, was I? I mean, would you? And all that tongue and groping was a bit of a diversion, so to speak. I rest my case!

So, our east coast surfari had to wait a little while as it took the cops two days to locate the van, and another three for us to hitch lifts to Broken Hill to pick it up.

It had ended up at the bottom of a small cliff, but luckily, it seemed to have survived the trauma and, once it had been hauled back onto the highway, we inspected the damage. It only sported a few dents and scratches and, of course, the concave roof from the earlier rollover, and a smashed headlight, broken radiator, and the bonnet wouldn't latch properly. But other than that...!

One rollover maybe, but a cliff dive as well was stretching it a bit for the old crate, and so it needed fixing up before we could continue on our surf odyssey.

Apparently, according to the cops, Brenda and Louise were not new to this sort of thing, and our bikini-clad Bonnie and Clyde had stolen cars many times before and even stripped and robbed a truck driver.

He was called Clive, and he had stopped to help them on an Outback highway when, once again, they claimed to have run out of fuel. One of them—probably

Brenda—tempted him out of his trousers with her ample assets and the promise of more to come, whilst Louise nicked his vacated undies along with his pants, which contained his wallet. On her signal, they both legged it to their stolen and adequately fuelled car, leaving him sans daks and jocks and with a bit of explaining to do to Mrs Clive.

"At least he'd have had something to remember them by!" said Gary, somewhat angry but forlorn. "They should make a movie about those two crazy chicks," he added. Maybe they will one day.

Anyway, back to the good old US of A.

At least we had *heard* of Las Vegas and so we thought we should do our best to enjoy it whilst we figured out how to get back to the coast. The Malibu Inn was in a seedy part of town and pretty run-down, but we desperately needed a place to crash, and so it would have to do.

We walked into the tiny reception area overseen by a plump lady with unkempt hair. She was wearing a dirty dress and had a cigarette hanging out of the corner of her mouth. She was sitting at a small reception desk located behind a glass screen which sported a sign saying *'Guns Must be Checked in <u>Before</u> Occupying Rooms. <u>NO</u> Exceptions'.*

What?

Unfortunately, even though we had no guns, our new friend insisted on giving us a rather thorough pat down and then searched our bags before she would confirm if she had a room for us.

"Guns in those bags?" croaked Mrs Grumpy whilst kicking my board bag.

"Surfboards," said Gary as if it should have been obvious to anyone with half a brain, which, not surprisingly, didn't help her mood at all.

She insisted on checking them carefully and, once she accepted that we weren't gun runners, she offered us a room on the first floor overlooking the pool for three dollars fifty per night. We bit her hand off and booked three nights for the discounted price of ten dollars. With these prices, we were beginning to like Las Vegas!

We piled our belongings into the tiny room, fell onto the bed and immediately descended into a restless sleep. You see, the air-conditioner rattled and hummed so loud that it almost drowned out the noise of the jets that, after taking off from the airport situated just across the highway, flew over the motel at about a hundred feet. Classy place was the Malibu Inn.

A mixture of jet lag and debilitating travel weariness meant that we slept, albeit fitfully, all through the night, only waking to the deafening sound of the six am flight to Chicago just overhead.

Clad in our boardies, we both ambled down to the pool to wake up and cool off. There was a high diving board, and seeing as me and Gary were pretty good at diving, we decided to put on a bit of a display for the guy cleaning the pool yard.

"Do that again and I'll kick you out!" was his critique of our considerable style. "Pool opens at seven am, or can't you read?" he shouted, pointing to a tiny, faded sign screwed to a veranda post at the far end of the pool.

"Sorry mate, we didn't know," I said meekly as he shuffled off in a huff. We assumed that he must be Mrs Grumpy's hubby.

A few minutes later, a tall guy aged around forty came down to the pool and started swimming laps. Mr Grumpy didn't challenge him and so we thought he must be a regular at the motel.

He introduced himself, and we reciprocated. "Name's Tom," he said in a rich, deep, West Coast accent that spoke to your soul. "You must be the two Aussie surfers that Rosemary was telling me about."

We could only assume that Mrs Grumpy's parents had not foreseen the woman she was destined to become when they bestowed such a lovely, sweet name on her.

"Yeah, that's us. You see, we were heading for Malibu and sort of got off course," said Gary to the puzzlement of our newfound friend. He told us that he had surfed Malibu and practically every other one of the Californian breaks many times over the years. He now lived in Hawaii. Jeez, Hawaii!

He was a really friendly guy, and he said that if we ever got to Oahu, we should look him up and he'd show us around. He told us that he was in Vegas for a convention and, later in the day, he was heading up to Lake Mead where he was meeting a friend who had a powerboat. He asked us if we would like to tag along and added, "Bring your boards, maybe we can try some wake-surfing."

Finally, water and waves—even if they were generated by a boat!

So after lunch at a nearby diner, we piled into his wagon with our boards and headed off on the thirty-mile journey to the lake.

We hurriedly unloaded the boards and stowed them in the waiting boat that was going to deliver our first 'surf' in what seemed like an age. It was a red and white jet-boat named *The Good Times* and was about twenty-five feet long and as sleek as an arrow. I was stoked!

Tom had a kneeboard that was probably four-foot six long and over two feet wide with a square nose and extra-wide tail. Strange looking thing but, hey, each to his own.

Gary has never been good in boats, and he didn't seem so happy with this one either.

"This boat isn't even a proper ski boat. It's too narrow and too amped up," he said with a furrowed brow.

I told him to stop worrying, and pretty soon we were out on the lake and picking up speed, with the wake producing a beautiful waist-high face. Gary still seemed a bit nervous and was holding on tight as we sped ever faster across the sparkling, vivid blue H_2O.

Tom asked if he could try out my board and then slid off the side, holding the tow rope until he picked up the wake like a pro. He was ripping and made it look so easy!

The Good Times was doing about twenty knots but not coping very well with the chop, and it didn't seem to like the crosswind that was now howling down the lake. Her super sleek lines were beautiful to behold, but a couple of times she literally left the water and became airborne!

I'd kneeboarded before, and Tom had said that I could try his board, and so I bumpily went over the other side with it. "Careful, bro', this boat is bloody dangerous!" shouted Gary, now looking pretty green around the gills, and hanging on as we pitched from side to side.

I was on my knees and bouncing around all over the place, struggling to get control of the damn board so that I could let go of the tow rope.

The Good Times was now heading straight into the west and so Nevada's huge afternoon sun was blinding me.

The board slipped from side to side on the face of the small wave, and I didn't have any way to control it. Tom was frantically waving at me and shouting for me to tie it or something.

Our skipper, distracted by our antics and the shouting, had to swerve to narrowly avoid a large tourist boat with the name *Moonlight and Roses* emblazoned on its side. At which point Gary was thrown from his seat, and I completely lost control and the board shot out from under me like a bullet. Caught by the slipstream, the oblong missile whacked Tom hard on the arm. We heard the crack over the noise of the engine, as he let out a long scream.

Next day, the story in the 'Las Vegas Sun,' summed up the incident. "Surfing icon and inventor of the Boogie Board, Tom Morey, was unable to appear at the American Surfing Association's annual convention today as he suffered a broken arm on Lake Mead yesterday. Initial reports claim that the injury was caused by a reckless Australian tourist attempting to water-ski."

Reckless? Water ski? Really? I was lucky I didn't break something myself!

Anyway, call himself an inventor, the stupid board had no fin for Heaven's sake! And it turned out that it wasn't a kneeboard at all and apparently Tom had been shouting to tell me to *lie* on it, not *tie* it.

In the end, he was pretty good about it all, but the news wasn't received very well by Rosemary, who was clearly an ardent admirer of our friend Tom, and so we got evicted from the Malibu Inn as undesirables. The 'Strictly No Refunds' policy was duly enforced and so, yet again, we were out of pocket with nowhere to stay.

Gary wasn't too happy with me either.

"That idiot skipper was going too fast and couldn't see a bloody thing because of the sun, and then he almost hit that other boat. I did tell you that the damn boat was dangerous, but you never listen!" said my best mate, turning the tables on me for a change.

That's rich coming from you, old Gary!

Anyway, he can say what he likes, but I say Don't Blame

it on The Sunshine, Don't Blame it on *'The Moonlight'*, don't blame it on *'The Good Times'*, but Blame it on the Boogie...board!

The Point

"This is daylight robbery, I should have that wave counted!" screamed Gary at the official, who was having none of it. I tried to reason with my best mate, and I agreed that it was a close call but, in the end, the judge had the final word.

I did tell him, but he never listens.

It's difficult to pinpoint where this all started, but it was probably when we first met Chaz.

It was in the pub, and Chaz was at the bar chatting to this gorgeous girl. He was wiry and tanned, had sun-bleached sandy-coloured hair that spoke of lots of time in salt water, and he was wearing a white T-shirt, blue jeans, and Desert Boots. A surfer, if ever we saw one.

We hadn't seen him before, and we knew almost every surfer from Trigg Point to Yallingup.

"He must be a blow-in," Gary and I chimed in unison and a bit too loud, because the stranger turned his head and looked us both up and down. He put his drink down, said something to the girl and then walked towards our now vulnerable-feeling location. He didn't look mean exactly, but he looked as though he could look after himself and, by the time Gary and I had looked around for an escape route through the crowd, he was upon us.

He stuck out his right hand and said, "Hiya fellas, mi name's Charlie, Charlie Hooper, Chaz t' mi mates," in a strong pommie accent. We both shook his hand and introduced ourselves and, at the same time, breathed a sigh of relief. He wasn't looking for a fight after all!

"Just mov'd intu a cabin in Miamee Caravan Paark. Only temporaaree like." So, he was, strictly speaking, a *local* then which, strictly speaking, we *weren't*.

"Sum bluddy graate surf braakes round 'ere," he chirped in his regional English twang. "Best fo' miles!"

We didn't disagree with that assessment and so spent the rest of the night drinking and exchanging life stories, which were mainly surfing-life stories. It turned out that he'd only been in the country a few weeks, and he'd come out to Australia as a fourth-year apprentice electrician but had decided to park the job for a while and just surf until his savings ran out.

"I didn't realise people surfed in Pommie Land," said Gary with a quizzical look on his face. "Too bloody cold, I should think, and no proper beaches."

"Yood be sirprysed pal, thas' peeple surfin' evryeewheres back home. Cornwall, Devon, Scotland, even bluddy Yorkshire neer whur I cum frum! I even think a young bloke surfed bluddy Blackpool a few years ago for Heaven's sake. Must have been a nutter!" he concluded thoughtfully.

I decided not to tell him who the young bloke might have been. Probably best to save that for another time.

We got on like a house on fire, and it wasn't long before he became our regular surf-buddy. We also introduced him to the delights of the Perth night scene, such as it was.

His good looks, broad accent, and easy-going, laid-back style made him an instant hit with the girls, and so we decided to hang onto his coattails, so to speak. Our dating success rate improved dramatically at Pinocchio's and, in fact, every nightspot that we frequented.

It was on one of those runs that Gary met a girl called Marlene and sort of started to see her now and again. Not really *steady* like, but they'd often finish up together at the end of the night for the 'smooch dance' and a bit of a pash outside.

Anyway, for a while, me, Gary and Chaz hung out together and, after a few successes in attracting the ladies and some great surf sessions under our belts, we started to call ourselves The Three Musketeers.

Corny, hey?

We ended up surfing with Chaz most weekends. He'd been

surfing all week whilst we were at work just dreaming about it, and so we were insanely jealous. And jealous of the fact that he was a really good surfer and much better than me, or even Gary.

It turned out that he was a competition winner as a junior and was sponsored by a local board maker in England called Cheater. Well, *sponsored* is a bit of a stretch from what he told us. All they did was pay his comp' entry fee, which was usually about a pound, let him ride a team board, and they gave him a T-shirt with their logo on it. Seems he did quite well and was winning a few.

Not much by the way of prizes though, except when he won the regional 'Under Seventeens County Championship' in Cornwall, for which he was awarded a new board. In fact, I think it was the board he was still riding. Cheater weren't happy because it wasn't one of theirs and so it stayed in the shed for a while.

After a couple of injuries and two or three losses, they dumped him from their 'team' and even took their board and T-shirt back. Jeez, those Poms were tight.

Chaz had a different surfing style to us. We had adopted the almost-sitting 'poo stance' in the bigger waves, and when we surfed our seven-foot-six 'shorties', but Chaz, on the other hand, was more upright which was similar to how I surf my longboard, or how they surf the big waves in Hawaii.

He'd take off, drop down the face, almost kneeling on the board with his back leg. He'd then drive the board up the wave, unleashing the power in his rear leg like a coiled spring. Wow!

So, he'd zoom out of those bottom turns, setting himself up for the glide or another drop and power drive. This was a good few years before Simon Anderson dropped the 'thruster fins' bombshell on the sport, which had, in some ways, a similar effect.

His board was a bit of a blast from the past, too. It was a pintail and just over seven-foot-six long, with two deep channels running parallel down the bottom either side of the stringer, and it had a really flexible single fin. It was a bit weird, but boy did he make it sing!

Anyway, one day out at Avalon Point near Falcon, Chaz was spotted by Cliff Forster, the local hero and Mandurah's only professional surfer at the time.

The surf was peeling off the point and producing line after line of clean, head-and-a-half high waves. Chaz was ripping! Me and Gary had scored a few nice rides, but we were really just left in his wake.

After a beautiful wave that provided Chaz with a three-second barrel, Cliff paddled over to him for a chat. He said that there was an amateur invitational competition on the following Sunday at Yallingup and he had a 'wild card' entry to give away, if Chaz was interested that is. Chaz jumped at the chance, and we were stoked for him too (if not a little jealous!).

So, on the Friday before the weekend of the comp', we decided to go into town and have a few celebratory pre-competition drinks, and all was going well until Gary bumped into Marlene—literally.

He'd first met her a few weeks earlier, and they'd hit it off. He saw her on the dancefloor and couldn't take his eyes off her. "Look at those beauties!" he kept repeating, picking out her crowning glories.

As I've said before, always been a boob man has Gary, and I put it down to the well-endowed Mrs Dobson, our first-year teacher in high school.

He'd never miss the English Lit class, and he always picked a spot where he could clearly see her considerable assets. He got really excited when, dressed in one of her usual far-too-low-cut tops, she occasionally dropped the chalk and then had to bend down to pick it up. "*Oh yeahhh…*" he'd whisper with a dreamy look in his eyes. Yep, been hooked ever since has my mate Gazza.

A few dances later and bit of pashing upstairs at Pinocchio's followed by some drunken wrestling in the back of his car, and he was smitten. Marlene was playing hard to get I think, and they were a bit of an odd couple. Gary being a skinny, grungy, albeit good-looking surfer, and Marlene thinking she was a supermodel. She was a big girl and, as Gary summed it up, "They're beautiful… er, I mean, *she's* beautiful."

Anyway, back to that fateful night in the pub.

"Right boys, what's it to be?" Gary enquired as he pushed his way through the crowd to the bar. Marlene had her back to him and, as usual when on a bar run, Gary sees nothing in his path and so he didn't notice who was blocking his way. He shoved past her, and she immediately let out a loud squeal as her Babycham cascaded down her ample cleavage. She spun around and, without looking, swung her handbag at the offending goon.

Gary, well-practiced in the art of dodging blows thanks to his mum's penchant for head shots as part of her corporal punishment regime, flicked his head out of harm's way.

Unfortunately, Chaz was just leaning in to shout his order into Gary's ear, and so he copped the full force of the heavy weapon just below his left eye. He reeled backwards and bumped into several nasty-looking characters, spilling their beers.

A scuffle broke out between two particularly drunk patrons who were convinced that the other was to blame. This brought in the bouncers who, using their own tried and tested way of diffusing the situation, started throwing punches at anyone within a five-yard radius. They then unceremoniously chucked the innocent out onto the street, whilst the guilty made their peace over a conciliatory pint at the bar.

Meanwhile, Gary was enthusiastically helping Marlene to dry her sodden boobies. She was clearly enjoying it, and the grin on her face suggested that these two might be getting, shall we say, closer.

I pulled him away from this clearly important and enjoyable wardrobe work and, between us, we managed to extract Chaz from the mayhem and into the relative quiet of the other bar in order to check out his wounds.

It wasn't good.

His eye was already beginning to close and showing all the signs of a real shiner to come. The corner of Marlene's bag had also carved a deep, but quite neat, two-inch half-moon cut to his cheek, and this was now sending a steady stream of bright red blood down his face and collar.

Oh dear.

Three hours later, we left the Emergency Department of Royal Perth Hospital with Chaz sporting six stitches in the wound and with strict instructions not to go in the ocean until they were removed sometime the following week.

"Wot am I goin' t' do about t'bluddy comp'?" lamented a downhearted Chaz as we headed for the train.

"Never mind, mate, with that eye you'd be useless anyway," suggested Gary supportively.

And so it was that Gary picked up the Wild Card for the 'WA Surfing Association Yallingup Invitational' from our new mate.

We slept in the back of my panel van parked just off the road and overlooking Main Break. You could hear the surf thundering onto the rocks and hissing like a steam train as it spent its power on the shallow reef below. It was going to be big, classic Yalls.

Gary was up with the first birdsong and sat cross-legged on the grass, gazing at the spectacle of awesome power that Mother Nature had set out before us. Poetic, eh? But that's what Yallingup does to you when it's 'on'.

Chaz had come along to support Gary and to explain his substitution to the flustered officials. That finally accomplished, Gary was registered and allocated to his first heat. To say he was nervous is a massive understatement and so me and Chaz did our best to comfort our little D'Artagnan.

I reminded him that he'd survived Ulus that time we were on the Isle of the Gods, well just; and there was the near drowning at Indijup when he couldn't get his head above the foam after a massive hold-down; or when he smacked his head on the reef at Avalon Point after spotting a two-foot fin close by; and not forgetting the rollover on the Nullarbor on our way to our East Coast Surfari.

He didn't seem particularly reassured by these reminders, even though, to me and everyone who knew him, he clearly did have this knack of coming out of scrapes largely untouched and, often, ahead.

Like the time that we were in California on our interesting, if not epic, Endless Summer surfari. We'd been sidetracked in Mazatlan, Mexico and in Las Vegas, and finally made it to Malibu.

As we walked through that famous entrance and onto the beach, we passed this gorgeous, blonde-haired and deeply tanned, bikini-clad girl selling hot dogs. Talk about a babe—you didn't find girls looking like that in Kelmscott, I can tell you!

I tried some of my inimitable Aussie charm on her, which seemed to work because she told me her name was Trudy, and she gave me extra onions and ketchup on my hotdog and didn't even charge me for it!

When you've got it, you've got it, eh?

"I reckon I'm in there," I said to Gary as we headed across the hot sand. "After we've had a surf, I'll turn on the charm, and she'll be putty in my hands. Yep, I'm on a winner there," I said confidently.

"*I wish they all could be California Girls,*" I hummed tunefully whilst munching on the hot dog as we passed through the gateway to the hallowed world of 'The Bu'.

Three-foot waves were peeling from way over in front of the lifeguard tower and running all the way across the bay to the pier. The longest right we'd ever seen, and boy did we want to get a few of those little beauties under our belt!

It was August and the sun was hot and so we grabbed our boards and charged into the water in just our boardies.

Big mistake.

It was probably thirty degrees air temperature and seventeen degrees in the water. Didn't see that coming!

Anyway, shivering, we paddled into the lineup and sat impatiently waiting for a wave that hadn't already been grabbed by one of the stylish locals. They were friendly enough when they found out we were Aussies but clearly hadn't quite got the 'sharing and taking turns' thing that we were used to at our home breaks.

Our chance finally arrived when a set came along that they all let go through to us. Maybe they were finally being generous, or perhaps they were just tired.

Who knows? Who cares? Let's go!

I paddled into the first wave of the set and took off on the glassy, chest high beauty that I managed to milk almost all the way to the pier, getting in a head dip and, very nearly, a cover up! I'd dreamed of this day since I was a kid dragging that old mal down the beach at Miami Bay, and I so was mightily stoked with my first wave at Malibu. As I turned around to paddle back out, I saw that Gary had let 'our' set go through and, seeing a bigger one behind it, he started paddling into a beautiful head-high screamer.

Unfortunately, he hadn't seen that Trudy, my sweet hot-dog-vending-beauty, was already on it and coming at him fast. She screamed at him something loud and very obscene (really Trudy, I thought you were such a nice girl!) and chopped a turn off the top of the wave just behind old Gazza. Her ten-inch fin missed his head by a fraction, thank goodness, but that wasn't the end of the drama.

Further down the line, she pulled off the wave and started paddling back towards where Gary was now sitting on his board, trying to regain his composure after the near-fatal collision. Still screaming at him, she was joined by two very unfriendly-looking dudes who were clearly the enforcers of their own version of Malibu surf etiquette.

Gary, always aware of his own strengths and weaknesses in such situations, realised he was likely to be in for a good thumping and so went for one of his little party tricks. He rolled his eyes up into his head, clutched his hands to his chest and let out a blood-curdling scream. He then slumped forward on his board, letting his head crash down on the nose.

Almost upon him, his three potential attackers stopped in their tracks and looked at each other, first puzzled but then, one by one, a look of horror spread across their faces.

"He's had a heart attack!" shouted the first local hitman on the scene. "I've seen it before. My granddad—he went down like a stunned bull in a slaughterhouse! Dead before he hit the ground." he added ominously.

A moment ago, his would-be attackers but now his rescue possie, the trio sprang into coordinated action.

Within not much more than two minutes, they were carrying Gazza up onto the safety of the beach and, by the time I arrived, 'my' Trudy was kneeling on the sand alongside him giving him mouth to mouth.

A couple of groans from Gary signalled that she'd brought him back from the brink and, smiling, she shrieked, "He's alive!" A round of applause arose from the small crowd of onlookers that had gathered to see what was going on, or to witness his demise, depending on your point of view.

Just then the lifeguard, who'd seen the drama unfolding from the tower, ran up to take control of the incident.

If I thought that Hot Dog Girl was hot, then this one was smokin'!

With flowing blonde hair and clad in a little red bikini that probably fitted her when she was twelve, she bounced across the sand and went straight into action, first checking

Gary's vitals and airway and then, sitting astride him, she leaned forward and looked deep into his eyes. "Can you see me, buddy?" she enquired in a perfect 'California Girls' accent.

"I, I, think so…" mumbled Gary, his eyes still fixed on the ample contents of her tiny bikini top.

"Wow, you're English!" she said excitedly.

"Nah, I'm 'straylian," was Gary's indignant reply.

"Australian…, oh, *niiice*," was her far-too-friendly response.

She didn't see the little wink he gave me as she slowly helped him to his feet and, putting his arm around her neck, she walked him up to the car park.

"My name's JJ, and next time you're at the Bu, be sure to call by Tower One and let me know how you are. Don't forget now…" she hissed sexily into his ear as she helped him into the car.

"Do all the lifeguards here run around in little red bikinis?" queried a triumphant Gary as we headed back to the motel. "I mean, it's almost worth drowning for! They should make a TV series about them; it'd be a smash hit!" he said enthusiastically.

Maybe they will one day.

So, yet again, Gary had avoided disaster by the skin of his teeth and come up smelling of roses. Yep, quite the Houdini was Gazza.

Now, where was I? Oh, yes, Yallingup.

Gary's heat was called and, wearing a red competition shirt, he paddled out to the line-up with three other hardy souls. The swell was already a good six-foot and building and had that surging power that the Southern Ocean often delivers to Yallingup. I could tell that Gary was nervous by the way he was paddling around, trying to get into a position of least risk, I surmised.

There were only a few minutes left in the heat, and two of the other competitors had already had a couple of good-scoring waves under their belts whilst Gary had only one mediocre wave.

For some unknown reason, this was the moment that Gary seemed to find his Zen. He was now sitting calmly looking towards the horizon as another set rolled into view. He let the first one go and then spun around and paddled hard as the second wave began to lift him skywards.

His take-off was perfect, and he slid to his feet like a cat, crouching low as he sped left down the face of the wave. He powered off the bottom and put in a succession of beautiful arching turns and cut backs, with the spilling wave almost slapping his shoulder.

This was Gary at his best!

As the lip of the wall of water began to pitch, Gary dragged his hand in its face, slowing just enough for it to spill over his head, and he disappeared into the 'Green Room'. Yes, he was in the barrel!

Everything went into slow motion for what seemed like an age before the wave collapsed and spat him out of the translucent tube like a bullet from a rifle.

Gary kicked out and paddled seawards, clearly knowing that he'd conquered the wave and, with it, his fear.

Me and Chaz were hooting and hollering and jumping up and down.

"That wuz a bluddy cracka' of a waave!" shouted Chaz above the din of the other applause and whistles.

There wasn't time for another wave for any of them, and the siren called them back to the beach.

Gary came second in the heat, and he could have won it if his first wave had scored a fraction more. But boy was he stoked!

"Did you see that wave, Ben? I mean, was that the best wave you've ever seen?" he kept blurting repeatedly as we congratulated him.

One guy had to scratch from the next heat due to a shoulder injury, and Gary had done just enough to scrape through to the final. Yes, the final! My best mate Gazza in the final of the Yallingup Invitational—surfing against some of the best in WA, including Cliff Forster! This was big.

And so was the surf.

It had steadily increased in size and power and by the time the finalists paddled out, it was pushing over eight feet with a stiff cross-shore breeze chopping it up.

We were all pretty quiet on the drive back to Mandurah that afternoon. Gary had done his best in the final, but the conditions and the strength and experience of the guys that he was up against had sealed the deal.

Chaz was trying his best to cheer him up, but it was a near impossible task.

"Bluddy graate pal, you were bluddy graate!" he repeated, but Gary was inconsolable.

"I was robbed, robbed I tell you, bloody robbed!" grumbled my best mate. "Why? Go on, tell me why? Zero, bloody zero, I scored in the final!"

"The official said that you took off on your one-and-only wave after the siren had sounded," I reasoned.

"Bollocks!" was his simple and succinct reply. "I'll never be able to show my face at the Surfing Association again!" he added bitterly.

"Surfing Association? Who do you think you are, bloody Cliff Forster? You've never even mentioned that mob before—always said you were a 'soul surfer'!" I retorted.

"And Marlene will think I'm a kook…" he whispered. "A bloody kook," his voice cracking with emotion.

He had clearly hoped to impress the lovely Marlene with his heroic exploits in the comp. He probably wanted to show her the results in the sports section of 'The West' the following Saturday, and brag about his epic performance in the huge swell.

"She'd think she was dating a movie star," mumbled poor Gary.

Dating? He really must be smitten!

He was inconsolable all week. He didn't even want to hit Pinocchio's on the following Saturday night, even though Marlene would, most likely, be there. As much as me and Chaz tried, we didn't seem to be able to lift his gloom.

"Might have finally got her to, y'know, do it," he said almost to himself when we did eventually catch up with him, finally admitting why he was so devastated. "Don't you get it? Don't you see?" he added with a questioning look on his face and the slightest hint of a tear in his eye.

"So that's what's eating you up! You want to get her into bed!"

Rather than his ego, it was his *virginity* that was the victim of his poor performance in the final heat of the comp. Poor bugger!

"That's not what I meant!" Gary was now almost shouting. "I meant, you know, go steady like. I think I love her, Ben."

So, finally, it's love, is it? Wow, my best mate going steady!

Seems like only yesterday that commitment just wasn't on the cards for old Gazza. He'd usually say, firmly and dismissively, that he just didn't see The Point.

Aloha, A Hui Hou, Mahalo – "Hello, Goodbye, Thank You"

"Aloha ʻoe i ko Hawaiʻi," said the beautiful Hawaiian girl as we descended the steps of the silver bird. She placed a lei made from frangipanis around my neck and then did the same with Gary. He flinched and craned his head away from the fragrant flowers, startling our welcome host such that she dropped the rest of the leis. She then set off in chase as they were picked up by the warm breeze and scattered across the tarmac.

You see, Gazza's hay fever could flare up at the slightest provocation, and so he was always really protective of his generously sized snout. Luckily, however, on this occasion he was fine, though I'm not sure the lovely wahine would agree!

We had started the day driving down PCH and CA-1,

flown from LAX on TWA in a 707, and landed in HNL. If you're confused, then just imagine how Gazza was coping with all the acronyms! "Bloody hell, Ben, I thought they spoke English in America!" was my best mate's confused comment.

This was meant to be our final stopping off point on the way home from our surfing odyssey, and it was a last-minute decision. After all, when was the next time we would have the chance to visit Hawaii and surf the breaks that we'd only read about in magazines or seen in surf movies?

We'd had a great time in So Cal, and things had gone really well for us when we finally reached the source of our boyhood surfing dreams. Well, mostly. There *was* the party in Zuma Beach that spiralled out of control and almost got us arrested…

You see, after Gary threw a fake 'near death' escape act followed by his subsequent and dramatic rescue on our first visit to Malibu, he became a bit of a celebrity there. "Go Aussie!" they'd shout, calling us into waves, probably to avoid another drama but, hey, at least we got to score a few beauties.

One of the Malibu locals, a guy called Brett, took a shine to Gary, and they'd spend hours in the line-up telling jokes and regaling each other with stories from Southern California and Western Australia respectively. I couldn't put my finger on it, but there was something not quite right about Gazza's newfound friend, but Gary just couldn't see it. He even invited Brett back to our motel for a few beers one time and, in the end, that proved to be a big mistake.

I did warn him, but he never listens.

Anyway, one day Brett invited us to a party that he was organising on the following Saturday, with lots of girls, beer, and music—you know, just right up our street! So naturally we jumped at the chance and noted the date and time, but we couldn't really pin him down on the 'where'. As the day approached, we assumed that our new mate Brett had changed his mind about our invitation as we hadn't seen or heard from him all week.

We were staying in a small motel called the Paradise Sands which was at Zuma Beach, another great surfing spot that was a short drive from Malibu. Saturday came and, after a cruisy afternoon surfing at Zuma for a change, we headed back to the motel, planning to have a shower followed by some food in the diner next door, where we'd decide what to do for the rest of the night.

As it turned out, our evening was already mapped out for us because Brett had hijacked *our* motel room for '*his*' party. We had no idea how he managed to get a key but there must have been fifty or sixty people split between the small bedroom and the pool area, and the music was blasting!

It looked as though the party had been in full swing all afternoon because most people were already drunk, and several of them were in the pool fully clothed.

Wasting no time to join the merriment, Gary screamed a

"Cowabunga", kicked off his thongs, and jumped into the pool to the cheers of the other revellers. Meanwhile, being somewhat less enthusiastic about joining the mayhem than my mate, I went to our room to search for old Brett and have a quiet word with him.

I stood at the open door for a few seconds, with my mouth also open, stunned by the scene before me.

There was a strong smell of pot mixed with stale beer, not a pleasant odour, and all of the girls were in tiny bikinis. Seven or eight of them were in the middle of the room gyrating their bodies rhythmically to the music of The Mamas and Papas.

I got dragged into the midst of the dancers and, before I knew it, my old friend Trudy, the 'Hot Dog Queen' from Malibu, appeared from the crowd and pulled my T-shirt off over my head. My puny, or should I say athletically muscled, torso seemed to drive the girls wild, because there were now three of my new scantily clad admirers taking turns at rubbing themselves against my naked chest and back. I was loving the increasingly intimate attention and one of the girls poured a bottle of sun oil over me to, shall we say, reduce the friction and increase the action!

Yahoo!

My board shorts were the next target of the manic mob, and my butt cheeks were hanging out from their drunken attempts at disrobing me. I was hopping around and desperately hanging onto the front waistband, trying to avoid revealing my underwhelming wedding tackle. Did I just say underwhelming? Well, these things were meant to happen in the dark, weren't they?

Their increasingly erotic and slippery assault wasn't going quick enough for Trudy, and to cheers from the crowd, she distracted me by removing her bikini top and then expertly yanked my boardies down around my ankles. This, not surprisingly, caused me to trip and fall flat on my face to the hoots and howls of the rest of the pack.

Aided by the lubricating action of the sun oil, I managed to escape Trudy's desperate grip which, in different circumstances, might have had a much more pleasant outcome. Momentarily free, I kicked my feet out of my trailing boardies, jumped up and bolted for the door before I found out what she and her frenzied followers planned next for my precious cargo.

Stark naked, and pursued by my delirious and whooping fans, I ran for my life. I managed to snatch up a swim-ring, in the shape of a large pink flamingo, that was sitting regally amongst the mayhem around the pool. I quickly stepped into it and, pulling it up around my waist to act as a makeshift loincloth, I sprinted breathlessly away from Trudy and the gang.

Having seen my manhood in all its glory, they were now standing in a line chanting melodically, "Ben's got no weaner, Ben's got no weaner, just like a ballerina!" at the top of their voices. Well, you see, just like a mountain gorilla, it always retreats into the forest when threatened. That's my argument anyway.

Was it a lucky escape from a fate worse than death at the hands of those crazed, bikini-clad beauties, or did I just miss out on the opportunity of a lifetime? I guess I'll never know.

Gary had been entertaining the throng in the pool with his broad Aussie accent and his ability to skull a pint of beer in one go, several times over. In the end, it was this latter skill that was his downfall, as it didn't take long for his new drinking mates to spot the impact of Gazza's overly stretched bladder on the colour of the pool water.

Within a few seconds and whilst shouting obscenities at my bestie, they all exited the increasingly yellowed water around him and started throwing the nearby chairs and loungers at poor old Gazza.

Luckily, he dodged the assault, and together we slipped away from the angry crowd and climbed nimbly into the sanctuary of the adjacent hot tub, which, to our surprise, was free from the marauding partygoers. We figured that there we could collect our thoughts and compare notes on our eventful evening so far.

The continuing mayhem didn't seem to please the other hotel guests, though, or the hotel manager for that matter, who was waving wildly from inside his office at the far end of the pool yard. To accompany his frantic hand gestures, he was screaming something through his window that we couldn't hear.

Meanwhile, a rather large drunk, with a full glass of beer still in his hand, was lying face down and unconscious right in front of the manager's door, which, unfortunately, opened outwards. Despite trying with all his might, the hotel official just couldn't shift the human doorstop.

Amazingly, not a drop of beer was spilled from the zombie's glass, despite him being repeatedly battered by the office door as the manager tried to escape. Clearly a highly skilled drunk.

It was then that we heard the sirens.

We jumped out of the hot tub and, someone must have waved a magic wand because the raucous crowd evaporated in less than two minutes. All that was left was me, still wearing the pink flamingo, Gary, now swaying from side to side as the effects of the copious amount of beer took hold, and the drunk blocking the manager's door. And, of course, a mess that resembled the Los Angeles County Garbage Dump.

The cops were very understanding once we'd explained that we were innocent travellers who had been hoodwinked by heinous and mischievous villains. They had broken into our room, stripped me naked, and thrown us both into the pool. They then pelted us with anything they could lay their hands on, so traumatising innocent little Gazza that he peed himself.

Well, it sounded more convincing at the time, and they liked our accents!

"My sister, Martha, lives in New Zealand. Do you know her?" queried the sergeant in charge of the surprisingly large law enforcement detachment. As we seemed to be ahead in the innocence stakes, we decided not to point out his geographical mistake.

Unfortunately, the manager didn't buy the story and

insisted that we left his hostelry, once we'd tidied up the mess that is.

Anyway, that's how we finished up homeless again and with some time up our sleeves, and so, rapidly running out of options, we decided to leave LA and do a stopover in Hawaii.

Once we'd collected our gear from the baggage carousel and cleared Customs, we exited the airport and stood in silence whilst gazing around and wondering what to do. Luckily, we managed to jag a lift to the North Shore of the island with a friendly guy called Henry. We bumped into him whilst trying to find a bus that would at least get us away from the airport and, hopefully, to a beach. He said that he had a shack at somewhere called Pupukea and he offered to let us bunk down at his place for five dollars a night. So, naturally, we bit his hand off.

It turned out that his shack was constructed from several sheets of corrugated iron that he'd nicked from a tin shed, some old doors, and a bit of palm thatch for the roof. The dirt floor had attracted its fair share of scary-looking bugs and, with an outdoor fire pit for a kitchen and no running water, it wasn't exactly what we expected for our five dollars.

He'd rigged up a sleeping platform to avoid the worst of the creepy crawlers that would just about take the three of us if we snuggled up cosily. As it turned out, it also provided a nice, dry resting place for the fleas and huge cockroaches that were everywhere in this corner of the Island of Aloha and that didn't seem to like the dirt floor either. These latter residents of our new abode showed no fear of humans and enjoyed sleeping inside our board shorts which, naturally, we wore night and day.

Despite its shortcomings, it was directly opposite the beach, and so we quickly settled into our new digs and spent the rest of the day sussing out the surf breaks.

To say that the surf looked challenging is a big understatement. It made Yallingup look like 'kiddie corner', and, to my terrified eyes, it had all the hallmarks of Uluwatu on steroids.

The next day me and Gary paddled out to the inside section at Pupukea and settled down to watch the talented locals put on a show on the 'real' waves that broke further out. These guys were good, and I mean good. With the memory of the Malibu debacle fresh in our minds, we spent a respectable hour patiently waiting.

Gary was the first to pick up a five-foot 'tiddler' that the local Hawaiians had turned up their noses at. My best mate put in a stylish ride, getting barrelled for a couple of seconds on the inside reef. This impressed a big Hawaiian guy called Willie, who was clearly very influential amongst the scary-looking locals.

He invited us to sit with them further out the back, and I managed to hide my jangling nerves long enough to pick up a couple of the smaller set waves that came through. I did OK too, thank goodness, including a cover up and a nice nose ride that drew some whistles from Willie and his mates. I felt like royalty!

These guys were really cool and took us under their wing, making sure we were able to surf Pupukea and nearby Haleiwa without getting harassed by other groups of locals. This benefit did, unfortunately, come with its drawbacks as they expected us to surf the same spots and tackle the same waves that they did.

Luckily, the swell was more or less manageable for the first few days until, that is, our new mate Willie announced to the cheers of his followers that "Sunset is going to be firing tomorrow", which I assumed meant that it was going to be big. Very big.

Gary, as usual, was really gung-ho and had more than kept up with them at Pupukea and Haleiwa, and so he joined in the cheering and enthusiastically agreed that we'd join them at Sunset. Naturally, my nerves didn't receive the news quite so well, despite all the excitement and multiple assurances from Gazza.

So, to avoid certain death, I feigned a hamstring injury, which was one of my favourite escape tricks. The following day, limping theatrically, I tagged along with the excited group and joined a fair-sized crowd on the beach to watch the spectacle that Mother Nature had arranged, all the while, massaging my fantasy injury.

I had no need to worry about Gazza as he acquitted himself honourably in the solid eight- to ten-foot waves, drawing lots of whoops and praise from the others. After a couple of hours and some impressive surfing, and now with a disappointed tone: "Not as big as I expected" was Willie's analysis of what, to me, was a huge swell on an increasingly scary-looking break. The wind had turned cross-shore and was now putting two-foot bumps on the turquoise walls which, sadly, put an end to Gary's fan club.

He struggled to stay on his feet whenever he took off on one of those corrugated mini-mountains, and so he eventually paddled in, exhausted and dejected, following several scary-looking wipeouts, and copious amounts of verbal abuse from Willie and the crew.

Oh how fickle fans can be!

So, we decided there and then that we should find somewhere with kinder waves and, perhaps, a new group of less demanding potential admirers. The following morning, we said our goodbyes to our landlord Henry and our cockroach friends and headed to the town of Waikiki in the south of the island.

We managed to get a bus from Pupukea, which took over three hours to reach our destination, but it was only a dollar each and so we couldn't complain. We got talking to a couple of guys on the bus who said that we should head for the Pink Frangipani Hotel as it was cheap, surfer-friendly, and only a few minutes' walk from the beach. Score!

They told us to get off the bus at Dukes Lane and ask for directions. So, after doing a couple of loops of the neighbourhood, we eventually found the Pink Frangipani and, sure enough, it wasn't half bad. Unfortunately, "Being half a dump is not much better than being a full one!" as my mate Gary pointed out philosophically when we entered our room.

We had booked into an 'Efficiency Room' which had tatty twin beds that had seen plenty of action, a rather tired and worn-out bathroom with a shower that dripped noisily, and a small kitchen that was probably home to a variety of vermin. Ah well, we reasoned, at least it was cheap and within walking distance to the beach.

We stored our stuff and then went back out to scout for the quickest way to the surf. We stood in disbelief as we watched the hordes of tourists on huge foam surfboards being shepherded around in the small inside waves by teams of Hawaiian beach boys. This was certainly no secret spot!

We got chatting to a Hawaiian guy at one of the beach stands who called himself Beaver. He looked about fifty but really athletic for an old guy. His dark eyes sparkled like Christmas tree lights, and the creases around them suggested lots of laughter. He had a quiet, confident demeanour that probably meant that he knew his stuff, and he talked us through the nine or ten outside breaks that were within paddling distance. Can you imagine so many surf breaks in one place?

He suggested that 'Queens' was a good starting point, and so we promised ourselves that's where we'd go at first light.

So, after a hamburger to beat all hamburgers from a street vendor on Kalakaua Avenue and a surprisingly good night's sleep at the Pink Frangipani, we grabbed our boards and headed to the beach. We consulted the map that Beaver had scribbled on the back of one of his leaflets and trekked a short distance south, down the ocean front.

The clear, blue water was like a warm bath as we paddled out to join around half a dozen locals in the lineup. It was perfect! An 'A Frame' was producing three- to four-foot waves with a short but punchy left and a longer rolling right. We had learned the local etiquette on the North Shore and so sat and waited patiently for the incumbents to give us the nod.

As before, once we'd caught a couple of waves that they'd ignored, and they saw that we were decent surfers, they signalled that they were happy for us to join the group and take our turn.

We had a ball, and Gary was on fire! His performance so impressed the only wahine in the lineup that she latched onto him and followed him around all morning. She was a beautiful local girl with long black hair and gorgeous dark eyes and, if that wasn't enough, she was an elegant and stylish surfer too. Just about perfect, I'd say! Her name was Kailani and the way she looked at my mate Gazza suggested that she was well and truly smitten.

The rest of the local guys were laughing at her antics, and I thought that maybe it was just a bit of jealousy. Score one for the Aussies!

After a clutch of great waves under our belts, we headed to the beach for a well-earned rest and some sustenance from a hot dog stand across the street. Gary wasn't trying to play hard to get with Kailani, but he hadn't fully latched onto her infatuation, and when I pointed out the obvious, he got really embarrassed. "Strewth, Ben, she's gorgeous. Do you reckon I've got a chance with her?"

His question was answered emphatically when we walked back onto the beach to retrieve our boards and his new-found admirer trotted towards him and pushed him back against a beach shelter. Looking over her sunglasses, and with a cheeky smile, she licked her index finger and drew a line down old Gary's bare chest and stomach, stopping just before it became an arrestable offence. She then whispered something in his ear that I could only guess at, but the expression on Gazza's face said it all. They arranged to meet that evening, and she said she'd be bringing someone else along. Score again!

So, after an afternoon of great surf, at the allotted time and suitably buffed and polished, we headed for the Outrigger Hotel bar to meet Kailani and her presumably gorgeous sidekick for drinks before hitting the Waikiki night scene. And then, who knows what love fest the night might have in store for us!

"Now, Ben, you'll have to look after her mate," said Gazza thoughtfully. "Kailani might just drag me off to somewhere, you know, more private and, well, anything could happen!" he said in a mock husky tone.

"Blimey, I don't like yours, mate!" Gary sniggered as we walked into the bar and spotted them in the far corner.

Kailani was looking beautiful in a traditional Hawaiian dress and with a frangipani bloom behind her right ear which I later discovered, indicated her single status. Absolutely gorgeous. Gary was in for a real treat tonight!

Standing next to her was her rather large, stern-looking wing-woman, dressed in what looked like an orange crimplene tent. She looked much older than Kailani and, as we approached, she sported a scowl on her face that spoke of much repressed anger. Kailani beamed a smile at Gary and then nodded an acknowledgement at me, as her friend stepped forward glaring at us, neatly blocking any approach to Gazza's beautiful admirer.

The night went downhill fast from there after Kailani, shouting over the shoulder of the human barricade, introduced us to her mum who, it seems, always insisted on chaperoning her darling daughter, particularly when she fraternised with foreign, haole scum like us.

Mrs Kailani had Gary tongue-tied within seconds as she fired questions at him like bullets from a machine gun. She obviously had a clear idea of the type of upstanding citizen that was suitable for her chaste daughter, and it took her no time at all to work out that Gazza definitely didn't fit the bill. He recoiled as she lunged at him, shouting angrily in Hawaiian, and it was only through some impressive and nimble footwork that he managed to dodge the copious amounts of spittle that accompanied the tirade.

Red in the face and her dress now looking like a deployed parachute, she chased Gary from the bar, screaming what were probably Hawaiian obscenities at the top of her voice.

Despite her considerable girth and the drag of the billowing fabric, she moved pretty fast, did Kailani's mum, and Gazza had to put on quite a sprint to avoid her clutches. Unable to run down her prey, she returned to the bar, glaring angrily at any shocked guest who happened to be in her path. Trying to look invisible, I stood motionless as she pushed past me and remonstrated noisily with her daughter. A minute or so later, and with a resigned expression on her face, the beautiful Kailani was dragged out of the hotel by her still frothing mum.

So, no passionate triste on the warm sand for Gary tonight, and no good-looking friend for me to charm. Just an excruciatingly awkward encounter with the local culture and an angry mum's puritanical views on the curse of sex before marriage!

The crew at Queens were still laughing when we saw them in the surf the next day. Gary got lots of pointing fingers, whistles, laughs and knowing nods, along with a few good-natured backslaps. All of which, no doubt, indicated that he wasn't the first poor soul to have fallen for Kailani's charms, only to have his ardour harpooned by Big Mamma.

Strange but true, and one could only imagine what the future held for the beautiful wahine when she finally escaped the shackles of her dear mother.

Gary was gutted and grumbled sulkily about his would-be lover for the rest of our time in Hawaii. Understandable, I guess, but it did start to grate on my nerves after a while.

Anyway, we finished our Hawaiian sojourn by surfing all the breaks that our new mate Beaver had suggested, including classics like Publics, Threes, Fours, and Kaisers.

A few days later, we departed the warm, surf-blessed 'Island of Aloha' aboard the Flying Kangaroo. After stops in Fiji and Sydney, we arrived back in Perth to an uncharacteristically cold and drizzly day. Thankfully, we were insulated from the chill by the warm glow of the memories of our many adventures.

"You know," said Gary as we descended the steps of the aircraft and still unable to let go of his disappointment, "I had high hopes for me and Kailani, but she never gave me so much as a Hello, Goodbye, or Thank You…!"

Serendipity

/sɛrənˈdɪpɪti /

Noun – the chance occurrence and development of events resulting in a positive or beneficial outcome

"It seems like we're always on the move these days," lamented Gary as we boarded the flight from Hawaii to Fiji on the next leg of our journey home. "Nothing ever feels settled," he added rather grumpily. He was right of course, but I didn't like to admit it.

We were now almost at the end of our three-month surfing odyssey which had taken us to Mexico, Las Vegas, California and, most recently, Hawaii. It had been an amazing adventure and, yes, we were ready to get home and settle back into a normal life, whatever that was.

Still, when the airline changed our return flights on us at the last minute, which meant that we'd have an enforced layover in Fiji for a few days, we jumped at the chance to add another destination to our trip diary. We'd heard that there might be some pretty awesome surf on the island and so we both agreed to make the most of the unplanned opportunity.

The flight from Honolulu was fairly uneventful, apart from right at the end when a passenger locked himself in the dunny and refused to come out even though we had started our decent into Suva International airport. We'd been diverted there from Nadi due to bad weather and the enraged passenger, who had availed himself more than heartily of the free on-board alcohol, slurred at the top of his voice that "Sshuva wassh not on tha bluddy itinererraaree," and, with a sweep of his arm, it was for him "Nadi or nuthink!"

The stand-off was finally resolved when a small Japanese bloke called Tsuyoshi, who was sitting close by, persuaded Wendy, the senior stewardess, to let him try to reason with the stubborn and increasingly petulant soul locked up tight in the cubicle.

After smiling sweetly at Wendy and the two other crew members who had arrived to help, he straightened his tie, wiggled his hips from side to side and then, screaming "Banzai!", he launched an almighty karate kick at the door. It smashed open, and the shocked, self-imprisoned occupant shrieked as he flung himself out of the path of the flying metal portal.

As the dust cleared and his screams subsided, the freed troublemaker stared incredulously at the pint-sized battering ram, who reciprocated with a polite bow. Instantly sober and too shocked to speak, staring blankly ahead he mouthed several expletives as he was escorted away by the cabin staff.

Tsuyoshi bowed humbly at the round of applause from the grateful passengers, and then quietly returned to his seat.

"Strewth, Ben, don't pick a fight with that guy!" exclaimed Gary, stating the obvious as usual. No mate, I don't think that that would be a good idea.

Crisis averted, the captain switched on the fasten seat belt sign and took us down for a bumpy landing on Runway One, well the *only* runway at Suva, actually.

With a five-day interlude on our journey home, we were going to check out if the rumours were true about Fiji having some great surf breaks. Of course, we had no real idea of what they were called or even where they were but, hey, we might never pass this way again and so what the heck!

We left the modest airport arrivals terminal expecting to find a tropical paradise with swaying palms and streets lined with colourful shops that were filled with friendly, grinning locals. It was a bit of a shock, therefore, to walk out into the oppressive humidity and a number of ramshackle market stalls that had been hurriedly assembled to catch the recent arrivals off guard.

A few rundown buildings, lots of potholes in the road, and a number of rusting old cars parked in the street added to this less than pretty vista.

"Maybe Suva town is much nicer," Gary said hopefully.

Hanging around the exit were half a dozen scruffy looking blokes who were aggressively touting their transport services with ne're a hint of a South Pacific Islander smile.

We escaped their clutches, and likely kidnap and possible murder according to Gary, and decided to head for a dilapidated-looking bus that was parked across the other side of a small square.

After a quick chat with Bruce the driver and following his good-natured assurances that he knew the location of the best surf spot in Fiji, we paid one American dollar each for the tickets to somewhere called Denarau, which was around four hours away on the other side of the island.

We loaded our boards and bags onto the already full-to-bursting luggage racks fixed to the rear of the bus and then climbed aboard. The bus was packed and so we ended up right at the back with a group of noisy locals that seemed to have brought along everything, including the kitchen sink. They were also accompanied by some of their precious and not-so-sweet-smelling livestock. The menagerie included a dozen or so chickens spread between several cages, all clucking and squawking noisily; a rather large and angry looking goat that was snorting and bleating loudly; a miniature pig that sat contentedly on his owner's generous lap; and two lambs that were clearly excited about their upcoming trip and so, baa'ing noisily, they gambolled up and down the aisle.

"Keep your eye on that bloody goat," said Gary. "He's a billy and looks to me like he's er, y'know, a bit frisky and looking for a girlfriend. He doesn't look too fussy either mate so watch yourself and, whatever you do, don't bend over!" he added with a hint of panic in his eyes.

No one else seemed to be phased by the melee, or the sheep and goat poo that was beginning to carpet the floor, and so we assumed that this was pretty typical of the local transport system.

Within a few minutes, the old bus chugged away from its resting place and headed northwest out of Suva towards the distant destination of Denarau.

We bumped along the rough roads, climbing towards a small mountain range that looked like a set from a Tarzan movie and, as the road got ever steeper, the groaning engine started to struggle. On the final stretch to the crest of the first high ridge, the bus slowed to a crawling pace and then spluttered to a halt. Shouting from his seat in the front, our still smiling driver, Bruce, told us all to disembark. We followed the crowd, who seemed to be used to the process, and shuffled off to stand in the warm, pouring rain whilst Bruce nursed the old crate up the final hundred yards or so to the crest of the hill.

At least we didn't have to push.

Having successfully ushered his flock back on board, we set off at breakneck speed on a white-knuckle ride down the other side of the mountain, flying through small villages and scattering animals and humans off the road in all directions. We assumed that the brakes weren't the strong point of the well-worn vehicle and so we both braced ourselves against the seat in front, hoping for the best but prepared for the worst.

This pattern was repeated several times on the remainder of the journey and, luckily, no injuries were sustained by the hapless residents as our jalopy sped through their hamlets. Well, not that we saw anyway.

On one occasion, just after we had hurtled through a small group of modest homes, and as if by magic, a ticket inspector appeared on board, complete with uniform and peaked cap. We first spotted him clinging onto the handle in the open doorway, looking a little unsteady with his jacket flapping in the slipstream. Moments later he was in the aisle, casually checking tickets. With a polite "Bula" and a wide smile that revealed sparkling pearly whites, he clipped our tickets, touched the peak of his hat in a respectful salute and moved on.

Distracted by keeping a close eye on the sex-mad goat and the piglet that had momentarily fallen from the knee of its now snoring owner and which had proceeded to take a pee on Gazza's shoes, we had lost track of the inspector. He was simply nowhere to be seen.

"Where the bloody hell is he now, and where did he come from in the first place?" queried a stunned Gazza. "I've heard about this stuff, you know, people appearing and disappearing before your eyes," he continued, convinced that there was voodoo at play.

We never did work it out and so were left to ponder the unfathomable Houdini-like puzzle and, perhaps, the wonders of the black art.

Needless to say, after another few hours fending off the amorous billy, which had definitely taken a shine to Gary, and the countless disembarkations whilst Bruce coaxed his charge up the hilltops, by the time we arrived at Denarau, our nerves were shot. We were both physically and mentally exhausted.

"Do we have to go back that way?" whimpered Gary mournfully as we unloaded our gear by the roadside. I just couldn't break it to him that there was only one road on this part of the island and so I decided to save that bit of news for later and, perhaps, when he'd had a few beers.

It was about ten pm and pitch dark as the bus pulled away from the spot that Bruce assured us was our destination. We quickly realised that we were, seemingly, in the middle of nowhere. In all the drama and excitement of the journey, we'd forgotten to check with our mate Bruce *exactly* where we were being dropped off and *exactly* where to find the surf that he had promised would await us.

Just when we were losing hope, a van pulled up, and the single occupant leaned over and, after greeting us with the obligatory "Bula", he asked if we needed a lift into Denarau. After explaining that we wanted to go to the nearest surf spot hereabouts, our new mate Danny the Driver advised us that Denarau had no surf, well none worth our time anyway.

Thanks, Bruce!

Danny said that there were big waves at some spots in the Mamanuca Islands which were only a ninety-minute ferry ride from Denarau. Unfortunately, he also advised that the ferry only ran twice a week, and we'd missed today's sailing.

Bugger!

So, dejected, tired and hungry, we agreed to pay him two American dollars to take us to the nearest bed and food. This turned out to be less than two minutes away in the centre of the village, which we hadn't been able to see in the pitch black of night. Scammed again!

The small guest house was just off the main street and, at four dollars for the night, it wasn't too bad. True, our room was pretty small, and the shared bathroom was outside at the back, but at least it was clean. There didn't seem to be too many bugs or mozzies around either, which was probably due to the several friendly geckos that shared our digs.

Unfortunately, there was only one bed and so Gary insisted that we slept head to toe, "just in case you have another one of those filthy dreams," he declared with a mixture of suspicion and disgust on his face.

As it turned out, we slept pretty well and after some breakfast, during which I broke the news to a very unhappy Gary about the transport links in this locale, we caught the same old bus back to Suva.

The return trip was every bit as hair-raising, just in reverse. Once again, the bus was packed, but this time without the animals thank goodness. We arrived back in Suva and got dropped off near to the centre of town, rather than back at the airport.

Here, we booked into a small hotel for our last few days in Fiji, dumped our stuff and then went looking for somewhere to revive our spirits. We found a lively bar close by, where we settled in for several cold Fiji Bitters to calm our frayed nerves and to recharge the batteries. We bumped into a couple of guys called Mike and Dusty who were also on their way back to Oz. They were from Sydney, and it turned out that they were keen skiers and often visited Perisher, a burgeoning ski resort in New South Wales.

Apparently, they had just been in Utah in the US at a ski resort called Powder Mountain and had been blown away by a new invention they came across there called the Winterstick. Basically, this was a fairly short and narrow wood and fibreglass board, turned up at each end. It was sort of similar to the deck of a skateboard crossed with a surfboard and was for 'surfing' on snowfields rather than waves. They reckoned that it was awesome and that a good surfer would pick it up in no time. Wow, trust the Yanks to come up with such a crazy idea!

"It'll never catch on. You'd have to be a nutter!" concluded Gary when our new friends went to the bar. "Too bloody cold for boardies so you'd need a two-inch thick wetsuit and even then, you'd still freeze your gonads off! Nah, just a stupid fad," he added dismissively.

Hmm, I had my doubts too, but stranger things have happened.

The bar quickly filled to bursting, and a band was playing some cool reggae music. It wasn't long before Gary was on his feet pulsating to the beat and getting up close and personal with a beautiful local girl. After a while, and for some reason known only to Gazza and the makers of Fiji Bitter, he dropped to his knees and started passionately kissing her bare belly button. Clutching Gazza's head and groaning in apparent ecstasy, she seemed to be quite enjoying the intimate attention being afforded to her navel. Unfortunately, her boyfriend wasn't quite so pleased.

He played lead guitar in the band and didn't seem to appreciate my bestie's rather obvious overtures, and so he jumped off the tiny stage and started swinging his six-string at Gary's head.

Gary ducked and dived out of the way of the musical missile, only to collide with Ronnie, the bass player, who had left the stage to try and restore some order, or to join in the fight—I wasn't sure which. As it turned out, he was doing his best to get his mate to calm down but alas, forgiveness was not in the air and so the jealous rage continued.

Faced with the prospect of a serious head injury, Gary bolted for the door and put on a sprint up the street, easily losing his pursuer, who stood waving his weapon in the air and shouting threats into the ink-dark night.

Calm was more or less restored when the rest of the band finally managed to drag their still angry mate back onto the stage to finish their gig, even though the beautiful Delilah had already picked another poor sucker to tease.

A lucky, if not rattled, Gary slipped back inside and hid

amongst the throng at the bar where he settled his nerves with several more beers. Not too long afterwards, the band, along with their resident temptress, departed for their next show elsewhere, and Gary was able to re-join me. Needless to say, he was pretty shaken by the unexpectedly scary welcome to the nightlife in Suva, and so he promised not to lick any more midriffs for the rest of the night.

This turned out to be a tall order as the Fiji Bitter flowed and the parade of beautiful girls on the dancefloor grew, tempting him back into the throng. He finally called it a night after whispering some not-so-sweet nothings into the ear of a gorgeous, slender beauty with long dreadlocks and ebony skin. She clearly didn't appreciate Gazza's dishonourable intentions and so almost decked him with a surprisingly powerful slap. With his head still spinning from the assault, and of course the beer, he staggered out of the pub only to fall flat on his face in the gutter where he spent much of the remainder of his second evening in paradise.

I did warn him, but he never listens.

It was in the same bar the following day, now filled with the sounds of steel drums and calypso music, that we by chance met another travelling Aussie surfer called Fred. He regaled us with stories of his travels whilst sailing his yacht solo around the South Pacific. He raved about Tahiti, which was still virtually virgin territory for surfers, saying that it had lots of inshore and offshore breaks that were as good as any in the world.

He'd also sailed through the hundreds of islands that made

up Fiji, including the Mamanuca Islands that our Denarau van driver friend, Danny, had told us about.

Apparently, there was a surf break there that rivalled The Pipeline in Hawaii. It was a huge, solid wave breaking over a shallow offshore reef and creating a long, left-hand barrel.

It was accessed by a small boat, and he painted a picture of his several surfs there so vividly that we almost felt that we were surfing it with him. The local name for it, roughly translated, was Thundercloud Reef, referring to the sound it made as it rolled over the coral below. Wow! And we were only a ferry ride away when we were in Denarau. Damn!

Ah well, it would have probably frightened the pants off us.

Fred then casually slipped into the conversation that there were a couple of good breaks around Suva that were well worth a look, including a right-hander called Suva Reef. This was near the lighthouse and only a five-minute boat ride from the harbour. What? So, we'd risked our lives to traverse the island on a dilapidated, six-wheeled rocket only to find that we could have stayed put and surfed in Suva!

Just our luck.

Anyway, the following morning, Fred met us at the harbour and took us out to Suva Reef on his surprisingly small yacht. The three of us had the break to ourselves, probably not surprising as surfing was still in its infancy in Fiji and visitors tended to head off for the more well-known and, perhaps, more reliable spots.

We didn't have any complaints though, as the tide was on our side and powerful four- to five-foot peelers were running along the reef. Perfect!

Fred was a good surfer, and you could tell that he'd surfed lots of different breaks in different conditions with varied power and size of waves.

Gary, of course, scored some blinders, and he and Fred were competing for the wave of the day. For this size of surf and bigger, Gary had developed a turn off the top of the wave which he copied from the likes of Michael Peterson, a surfer from Queensland, who was turning the surfing world upside down. Gazza hit the lip almost vertically and spun his board almost one hundred and eighty degrees to shoot back down the face and carve an arching bottom turn, setting up for another lip-smashing. It was awesome to see, and he just got better and better as the day went on and as his confidence grew.

I had my fair share of crackers too, with one beauty that I picked up just as it peaked overhead. I shot down its face like a rocket, putting in a series of neat bottom turns and tight re-entries. I was almost kneeling as the lip pitched over to form a perfect tube. Yes, I was in the barrel and flying along like a jet plane. Woo hoo!

When the wave finally spat me out, I was crouched so low with my head virtually between my knees that I didn't see the young grommet who had decided to join in the fun. He was paddling into the lineup on an ancient-looking and battered pin tail that was around six foot six long.

The kid was now dead ahead of me, and I screamed at him hoping he could understand my rantings and roll his board or dive below the surface to avoid the looming calamity. With a panicked look in his eyes that could have graced the screen in any horror movie, he dived off his board and, thankfully, was just deep enough for me to miss him.

Human crisis averted, I couldn't avoid running straight over his board, my fin cutting a neat rail to rail slice that almost chopped it in half.

Despite his lucky escape, our new acquaintance, Samu, wasn't happy and was now screaming at me. I was just about to point out to my young adversary that I had right of way, and that he had survived a potential disaster due to my clear, life-sparing instructions. However, I thought better of it when his big brother appeared and paddled over to join the debate.

When I say big, I mean big.

He was built like a sumo wrestler, and he looked as though he could crush a golf ball in his bare hand, like Odd Job from the James Bond movie, *Goldfinger*. I'm also sure that he would have easily held his own, and very probably prevailed, in any dispute with a bunch of angry locals on the North Shore of Hawaii. As long as there were less than ten of them, that is.

"Keep your mouth shut, Ben, remember what not to do with an angry bear," I repeated to myself several times.

In the end, my submissive behaviour and pleas for mercy, coupled with an offer to get the board repaired, even though I thought that it would probably cost more than the antique was worth, I eventually managed to pacify them both.

My nerves were shredded and so, after I'd put Samu's damaged board in the boat, I sat out most of the rest of the session with only a couple of other waves to add to my earlier tally.

Fred returned us to the harbour, and after some food and a few calming beers, he introduced me to Rizza, an old sea dog that had settled in Suva and who doubled up as the local board repairer. Actually, there wasn't much demand for board repairs in this almost surfer-free part of the world, but he fixed boats and so had the necessary skills with fibreglass and could manage, well, virtually anything made of that particular toxic material.

"Should take me a couple of hours," estimated the board doctor, "and it'll be just like new," he added. I admired his optimism but doubted whether he could fulfil such a promise, given the thing only looked fit for the garbage dump. I slapped myself at that unkind thought; after all, any surfboard was rare in these parts and would be priceless to the person who owned it. I knew from his reaction to the damage that I inflicted that Samu's beat-up old board was like gold to him, and so I felt guilty for decrying it.

Rizza set about his surgery on the board, whilst humming some indecipherable tune to himself.

It was difficult to guess his age but from his creased, leathery and weathered face, which spoke of much time at sea in the tropical sun, he looked about fifty. He could have been much younger or older, but I've never been good with people's ages. Unusually, he sported pierced ears with large loop earrings in his earlobes, a straight-through nose piercing, and a pin through each nipple. Ouch! We'd never seen anything like this before, and so me and Gary had trouble not staring at his body décor.

As we watched him work with the board, I noticed that he had a pronounced groin twitch. You couldn't miss it, and it seemed to become more exaggerated as the afternoon wore on.

We found out later from Fred that it was rumoured to be the result of another piercing gone wrong. Never one to turn down a dare, Rizza's mates had challenged him to add to his visible metal decorations with one located in that unspeakable spot that makes us blokes wince at the very thought.

One night whilst leaving a particularly seedy bar near the docks in Hong Kong, Rizza spotted a sign over a dingy-looking door that read 'Petra's Perfect Piercings. Satisfaction Guaranteed or Your Money Back'. Egged on by his sniggering shipmates, he entered the not-so-salubrious salon.

Petra, belying the image conjured up by her sweet name, was a one hundred kilo ex-truckie from Queensland with bad breath. Apparently, bored with her life on the road, she had stowed away on a tramp steamer and left Townsville in search of her dreams. A vigilant crew member found her the following day, camped out in one of the dodgy-looking lifeboats, complete with all her worldly goods and her dog.

Bluey, the Jack Russel terrier, became an instant hit with the captain when he demonstrated the hunting skills common to his breed by chasing down a huge rat that had taken up residence in the skipper's boudoir. It took the pint-sized pooch but a few seconds to end the rodent's reign of terror, thereby winning the skipper's heart and a free passage for him and the lovely Petra.

Little Bluey seemed to enjoy his allotted role, but he certainly had his work cut out keeping the abundant rat population under a semblance of control. Petra worked her passage as relief crane operator, unloading cargo when Mervin, the incumbent heavy equipment technician, was too hungover to properly carry out this vital function.

A few weeks later, she disembarked the vessel in Hong Kong under something of a cloud following an unfortunate incident at their previous port of call, which was North Harbour in Manila.

It seems that, on the wrong side of a bottle and a half of rum which, to this day is still her usual mid-morning tipple, she mistook the Harbour Master's office for one of the three flat-bed trucks that were waiting for their cargo of pig iron. The once tiny but proud mock-colonial style building now resembled a bomb site, and it took some time for the rescuers to free the unfortunate official from the rubble. He was, thankfully, unharmed and, in the confusion, the *SS Mount Isa* quietly slipped her moorings and sneaked off into the darkness of the South China Sea.

Needless to say, Petra was removed from crane duties and spent the rest of the trip cleaning the crew's ablutions.

Having discovered that operating a crane was not top of her list of abilities and as she was not enjoying her current assignment in the dunnies, on leaving the floating rust bucket she resolved to search for another and, hopefully, less demanding and more fulfilling vocation.

She had done needlework at primary school and so, a few weeks after arriving in Hong Kong, she jumped at the offer to work in a tattoo parlour. It was in Lockhart Road, in the middle of the city's red-light district, near where she was working as the bouncer in a brothel.

Unfortunately, it turned out that artistic skills weren't her strong point, and so she only lasted a day as a tattooist before a complaint from a particularly irate customer drove her from her new career. Apparently, his intended tattoo of an American eagle so closely resembled Donald Duck that he had to have it coloured in, just as Walt Disney intended.

Not to be beaten by this minor setback, within no time at all she set up shop in a tiny, poky room close to the docks to try her hand at the new and increasingly popular fashion fad of body piercing. "Business has been a bit slow," lamented Petra, but I'm hoping my work speaks for itself."

As he stood in Petra's newly occupied premises, Rizza gazed around at the scruffy and dilapidated, musty-smelling room. He was beginning to regret his earlier bravado and, with his grinning mates blocking any tactical and diplomatic withdrawal from his drunken stupidity, "Please, please be gentle," he begged nervously as he laid his wedding tackle on the table. Smiling and nodding reassuringly, Petra used a bike pump to prime her homemade pneumatic piercer.

"Hold still and you won't feel a thing," she hissed through ill-fitting dentures. She peered over her huge chest at his shrivelled sausage, holding it firmly between the stubby fingers of her left hand.

Her amateur dart gun let out a loud 'duff' and Rizza screamed one of those piercing screams (pardon the pun) that speaks of mind-numbing agony.

"You moved, you bloody idiot!" Petra bellowed as she grappled with her patient's parts, accidentally firing off two more shots from her patented piercer. With her last attempt before she needed the bike pump again, she finally hit the 'X' that she'd drawn in blue biro precisely half an inch from the tip of his wotsit.

Rizza screamed repeatedly as he rolled around on the floor, delirious with pain and cradling his badly swollen weaner, which now sported four studs in that most tender region of his being.

His recovery was, we were told, understandably quite slow, and it was some time before he could even talk about his ordeal without turning ghostly white and screaming uncontrollably again. This was despite the fact that Petra had honoured her advertised pledge and refunded his ten Hong Kong dollars in full.

"I could have charged him forty dollars for the four studs, you know," she said haughtily, "but it's not all about the money. I'm an artist after all," she added.

Rizza insists that after a few weeks, the antibiotics completely cleared up the nasty discharge and that, eventually, things got back to normal in the bedroom department. His wife Rita (Rizza and Rita?) was, apparently, a little happier too. "He doesn't seem to have as much trouble with our intimate relations now, thank goodness," she said some months after his ordeal. "Particularly since I got the magnet."

Hearing the story had us in fits of laughter with tears streaming down our faces, whilst, not surprisingly, clutching our privates protectively. For days after Fred had shared the story with us, we'd burst into giggles as random thoughts or occurrences brought back the images of old Rizza's torturous experience.

Definitely one for the travel diary, and me and Gazza lived off that story for quite a while, I can tell you! Of course, it got increasingly graphic and exaggerated as time went on and as the audience and the circumstances allowed.

We duly compensated Rizza with American dollars for his work, and with copious amounts of beer for the many laughs that his story was bound to give us.

Thankfully, with Rizza's expert care, Samu's battered board was suitably fixed and returned to its owner, and Odd Job was appeased to the point that his 'contract' on me was withdrawn. Phew!

Our time in Fiji proved a bit of a life lesson for me and Gary as we quickly realised how fortunate we were to live in The Lucky Country.

Lucky indeed. We had shoes, a change of clothes, homes with inside dunnies, jobs, and money for food. None of which, we discovered, were guaranteed hereabouts, and it was highly unlikely that there'd be anything left over to buy a surfboard, whatever its condition.

In the short time that we had left, we saw more of our two new local surfing friends, Samu and his big brother Maciu. Once they realised that we were only ordinary dudes and that we were respectful to them, their country, and their surf breaks, we got on OK. It turned out that they were orphan brothers who were scratching an existence by working on local fishing boats when they were lucky or cleaning out septics for the more well-to-do in the posher neighbourhoods when they weren't.

No dole here, just the stark realities of survival.

They were in between jobs at the time—the septics take a while to refill, I guess—and so we shared a few more nice surf sessions at Suva Reef.

After our final chilled-out afternoon session, the brothers invited us back to their tiny pocket-sized shack to recuperate with a couple of beers. I was surprised to see that Samu, who was probably only about fourteen, was also on the Fiji Bitter and he was easily keeping up with the rest of us. Different strokes, I guess, but I couldn't help wondering what lay ahead for him in the undoubtedly hard years to come, and what part alcohol might play in his potentially bleak future.

Leaving Fiji was sad, not so much because of the great surf that we'd enjoyed, or the friends that we'd made, or the heart stopping experiences we'd had going to Denarau and, for different reasons, meeting Samu and Maciu, but rather because this was really the end of our international surfing adventure.

Only a pit stop in Sydney and a windy touchdown in Perth were now between us and a shock dose of reality.

Before we knew it, we were back at work punching the clock and desperately wishing its hands would move quicker so that the weekend would arrive, and we could sniff freedom again.

Although not consciously, I don't think that either of us ever took things quite so much for granted as we'd done before. Whether it was the abundance of surf breaks on our doorstep, the boards we rode or the clothes we wore, the friends and family that we had, or even the food we put in our mouths three or four times a day.

Our few days on the island gave us highs and lows, much laughter and a few tears, excitement and fear, friends and foes but, above all, it helped us realise just how amazing our lives were back home.

Yes, our trip to Fiji was an unplanned and unexpected happening that gave us some great surf sessions and taught me and Gary a few lessons in life that were, in a way, in a good way, life altering.

True serendipity.

Or maybe we were finally growing up? I'll let you decide.

All Surfers Great and Small

The screech of burning tyres pierced the air as the Flying Kangaroo touched down.

"Welcome to Perth where the time is two pm and the temperature is twenty-eight degrees," announced the flight attendant over the PA system. "Please remain in your seat with your seat belt fastened until the captain has switched off the seat belt sign," she continued, ending another episode in our search for surfing Nirvana.

Gary and I had had some great adventures, and quite a few not so great, but this one had been a doozie.

We'd spent over four weeks making our way from Perth to Noosa and back but, as it turned out, the trip hadn't started too well.

We'd driven my trusty panel van across the Nullarbor only to have it stolen at Cocklebiddy Road House by two very attractive, bikini-clad hoodlums. It got pretty well trashed before we managed to recover it in Broken Hill.

The mechanic at the repair shop didn't pull any punches. "It's a pile of crap mate and not worth repairing," he reported in a slow drawl. Must be from Queensland, I thought, as he ran through the long list of repairs needed to make my much-loved set of wheels roadworthy again. I couldn't bear to listen, but my ears pricked up when he said it would cost almost two hundred and fifty dollars to get it back on the road. Two hundred and fifty dollars?

I thought about ringing my dad to ask him to loan me the money but remembered that I already owed him nearly as much for the new garage door that he'd subbed me for...

You see, I'd been out with a girl called Francesca who had decided to give me a second chance after our disastrous first date, during which I'd managed to get us thrown out of Pinocchio's. It's a long story but, suffice to say, there were a few too many Swan Lagers, copious amounts of vomit, and some angry bouncers involved. Not pretty.

It took a while for her to come around, and I think I was in the right place at the right time when she was on the rebound after her new boyfriend had dumped her. Apparently, she had started to talk about weddings and commitment and stuff and, understandably, he bolted. Well, who wouldn't?

We'd been out for a few drinks in Mandurah and then parked at the beach until past midnight for a bit of pashing and groping, before I reluctantly took her home. I pulled onto the driveway and expected to just drop her off, but she seemed to be determined to pick up where we'd left off at the beach. Things started to get pretty steamy very quickly I can tell you and, within seconds, she was straddling me in the driver's seat and taking off her blouse. I fumbled with her bra clip and fought for air as she locked her lips onto mine, like a limpet on a rock.

Just as we were about to move our fledgling relationship up a notch, there was an almighty banging on the roof.

The engine was still running (my first mistake), and it was still in gear with my foot on the clutch (my second mistake). Well, it had all happened so fast, and Francesca was clearly pretty determined to rid herself of the memory of whatever-he-was-called, and so she wasn't going to waste any time.

I rubbed away the condensation from the side window (my third mistake) only to see her dad glaring at me with that 'I'll rip your throat out' look in his eyes. He must have heard us arrive and decided to see what we were up to on his driveway at one o'clock in the morning.

As the panicked Francesca launched herself off my lap and scrambled back into the passenger seat whilst struggling to get her bra and blouse back on, my foot slipped off the clutch and we lurched forward.

The loud crash confirmed the outcome. The brand new, freshly painted, state-of-the-art, up-and-over garage door was now a mangled wreck. Luckily, this distracted her dad's attention long enough for Francesca to finish getting dressed and get out of the car, and enough time for me to reverse my miraculously undamaged van off the driveway and hightail it home.

Not that her dad forgot it or forgave me. In fact, if I were to believe his threats, I had better make sure I never crossed his path again, or Francesca's.

I did the right thing of course and offered to pay for the damage, even though I didn't have the money, but I managed to persuade my dad to lend me enough to appease Mr F's wrath. There was, therefore, no chance that my dad would come to the rescue now, and so it looked like me and Gary were stuck in Broken Hill.

The mechanic said he'd give me a hundred and fifty dollars for the van, which he could use for spares. Was he joking? A hundred and fifty dollars for my passion wagon; for my freedom chariot; for my surf-mobile? Just when we thought all was lost, he said that he happened to have a rather dilapidated looking Kombi van available, that was licenced and ready to go, for just that amount. What a coincidence!

As it turned out, the Kombi didn't look too bad, and at least it would fit our boards and swags and, with my foam mattress, we'd be able to sleep in it.

It was hand painted a sort of earthy brown colour which probably covered up its true condition, but the engine sounded sweet to my inexperienced ears, and it was blowing no smoke. So, we loaded our gear into our new not-so-trusty-steed and set off from Broken Hill.

We headed across country via Wilcannia, Mullengudgery, and Dubbo, arriving at Port Macquarie after two full days of driving.

Yes, we'd missed out Sydney's Northern Beaches, but we'd chewed up so much time with the whole 'Brenda and Louise' debacle on the Nullarbor that we had to sacrifice something, and we were determined to make it to Noosa.

For our first night on the coast, we camped in the caravan park at Crescent Head.

We woke to head-high waves peeling off the point with just two other souls out enjoying the classic break. We threw on our boardies, grabbed our boards and spent the next three hours racking up a hefty wave count.

Gary was on fire, scoring a beautiful four-second barrel on his second wave, and so he was stoked and whooping like a banshee for the rest of the session! I managed one of my best surfs for a very long time, with a couple of cover ups and more head dips and nose rides than I can remember.

We staggered back up to the Kombi, stored our stuff and headed to the camp kitchen where we cooked up the eggs and sausages that we'd picked up en-route. Topped off with toast cooked on the barbie and a mug of tea, we were stuffed!

We managed another two surfs on that first day and also had the following day full of joy supplied by Mother Nature. We were sorry to leave Crescent, but our next stop was Byron Bay, and we were anxious to get there and sample its fabled delights.

A guy that we met in the Crescent Head RSL tipped us off to a secret spot a bit further north that was on our way to Byron. It was called Trial Bay, near South West Rocks, and so we risked a diversion from our quest and, after an hour or so, we swung off the highway to find it.

You have to drive past the old jail, which presumably gave the place its name, and through a caravan park to get to the beach which swept away to the north to form a huge bay. The southern end was protected by a long, narrow finger of rocks that poked out into the Pacific Ocean forming a giant breakwater.

A huge south easterly swell was pounding on the rocks and, from there, clean three- to four-foot waves were wrapping around and peeling for what seemed like a mile across the wide bay. There was no one else in sight and I couldn't wait to get in, managing to beat Gary to the line-up by a good five minutes.

He paddled past me and out into the centre of the bay, which was picking up more of the swell and this was now producing a five- to six-foot 'A Frame' that thundered down the middle and almost all the way to a small river mouth. Typical of Gary to go for the biggest and gnarliest wave, but boy did he have a ball!

I had my share of crackers too, with one wave that I swear I rode for almost a quarter of a mile, stepping off on the beach and needing more than a ten-minute walk to get back around to the paddle-out point. By lunchtime we were tired out and decided to get back on the road so that we could reach Byron in time for a late afternoon surf.

It was just before four o'clock when we pulled into the car park overlooking The Pass. We unloaded our boards and wasted no time joining another six or eight guys in the line-up, where they were enjoying chest-high peelers that were wrapping around the point.

After a couple of hours or so, and more than a baker's dozen each under our belts, our spaghetti arms forced us to retire for the day. We weren't able to camp in the car park as we were told that the ranger and the cops were pretty active after dark. So we set off to find a campsite and managed to book into the Rising Sun Park, which was just off Lawson Street in the heart of the small town. It was right on the beach in front of the remains of a shipwreck, which gave the break situated right out in front of the caravan park its name. Score!

A good feed at the Byron Bay Hotel, followed by a few beers, put us into an early bed and we slept like logs until dawn.

After a quick freshen up, we drove south around the headland to Wategos and surfed a few nice two-foot waves until hunger set in and we retired to the Kombi for some breakfast.

We stayed a couple more days, savouring the delights of Byron by day, surfing the Wreck, the Pass, Wategos and Belongil, and also venturing to Broken Head, which was just a few miles down the highway. By night we split our time between The Byron and the Northern.

Both served ice cold beer and cheap, good food but The Byron won the prize for the number of good-looking girls.

Gary had suddenly become a bit of a reluctant wingman for some reason and so put a bit of a brake on my progress in the passion department. Perhaps he was thinking of his new infatuation with Marlene back in Perth—a bit out of character and very inconvenient I have to say—but I managed anyway!

After Byron Bay, we called in at Cabarita to check out the bay and then Currumbin, just an hour or so up the coast, where we surfed The Alley. From there it was a four-hour drive to Noosa, our dream destination.

We rolled down Noosa Parade and into Hastings Street and headed to the General Store for some provisions. There wasn't much else on Hastings Street, just a butcher, a real estate agency, and a few other low-rise buildings and, of course, the Surf Club at the far end of the street, near to the soon-to-become-famous First Point.

We managed to jag a spot to park and bed down for the night just up the road at the National Park, where we were tucked away at the very top of the dirt car park. With no lights on, a moonless sky and the brown paint on the Kombi, we were virtually invisible, and so we didn't get disturbed by the ranger. It was a different story the next night, and so we managed to find a campsite that fitted the bill by the river in Tewantin.

We woke after our first sleep in Noosa and found that the break out at the front of the car park, known as National Park, was firing! We downed a quick breakfast of cornflakes and bananas and headed out. Scrambling over the rocks, we couldn't believe our eyes. There was a solid three-foot swell with lines all the way to the horizon, and no one else out!

The glassy, shoulder-high waves were wrapping off the boulders at the point, and we surfed all morning, racking up some of the best rides we'd had in a while, not counting Crescent that is. I caught a beauty that linked up all the way through Little Cove and around to First Point. It took me ages to paddle back around to Nationals but, boy, was I a happy chappy!

As the tide changed and the swell dropped, we crawled back up the now urchin covered rocks to the Kombi, sunburned, exhausted, but unbelievably stoked.

We drove down into town and grabbed a Mega-Burger and chips from the General Store. We gobbled down the delicious food whilst sitting on Main Beach and watching First Point as it turned almost flat.

Mega Burger it was, because we were so stuffed that we couldn't have walked out to the point never mind surf it! We lay in the shade of a tree on the warm sand, gurgling and burping, until we both slipped into a sound surf-stoked sleep.

We woke up a couple of hours later to see that First Point had come alive again with the incoming tide, and so we grabbed our boards and joined the line-up. Three hours later and more little sliders than we could count, we headed back to the campsite for food, rest, and then a few beers in the Royal Mail Hotel in Tewantin.

This became our routine for the next six or seven days,

with the addition of fitting in an early afternoon surf at Little Cove, also known as Johnson's, which was sandwiched between National Parks and First Point. We also took the long walk around to Tea Tree Bay several times to enjoy its picture-perfect location and awesome, consistent chest-high peelers. It doesn't get much better than that!

We decided to explore a bit further north and discovered North Shore, which was a short chain-ferry ride across the Noosa River, and then a five-minute drive to the beach, which was accessed through a campsite. No one else but me and my best mate, chest to head-high waves, warm sunshine, and gentle offshore breezes all day long. This really was our Surfing Nirvana.

We came, we saw, we conquered!

All good things must come to an end and so it was that we had to drag ourselves away from Noosa and start the long journey home. We had hoped to get up to Rainbow Beach and surf the fabled Double Island Point (or 'DI' as the locals called it) that was discovered by Bob McTavish and George Greenough in the early sixties, but we had run out of time. Maybe next time.

We planned our route back to Perth, figuring that it would take us another seven or eight days of hard driving to get back, and so, at first light, we set off south towards Caloundra before heading southwest across country towards a distant Port Augusta via Beerwah, Dirranbandi, and Goodooga.

And then it happened.

After two and a half days of driving, we'd just entered Broken Hill (again...) and the Kombi blew a piston. Or at least that's what the mechanic, who originally sold us the van, told us when we finally managed to track him down at the pub. This was the death knock for the Kombi as it would need a full engine rebuild which would cost too much and take too long.

We managed to negotiate with our mechanic friend the princely sum of one hundred dollars for it which, given that we only paid him a hundred and fifty, was pretty good. Or had we just been conned? Anyway, we took the money and started to figure out how to get home before we got fired from our jobs for being AWOL.

Lady Luck must have been smiling on us because we managed to get a lift on a truck that was heading to Kalgoorlie in WA, which was only six hundred kilometres from Perth. The driver was Scottish with an accent so thick that we could hardly understand a word he was saying, but he was friendly enough and the journey wasn't too bad. We managed to fit our boards on the back of the truck, thank goodness, and we'd salvaged our sleeping bags from the van. There was plenty of space in the big truck and so we were able to stretch out and sleep quite well.

We arrived in Kalgoorlie after two full fifteen-hour days of solid driving. How do the truckies do that?

After one night in Kal, we learned the hard way that we had to get out of there, and fast! The locals and the miners took partying to a whole new level, and we just weren't up to the challenge. "Effing lightweights!" the patrons of one bar screamed at us in unison (and not so politely) as we scrambled out into the street, drunk and incoherent, escaping yet another drinking challenge.

The hundred dollars that we got for the kombi just about covered two air tickets back to Perth and so the last leg of our journey was quick and stress free. We'd had a huge adventure and, finally, managed to fulfil our dream of an East Coast Surfari. Well, most of it at least!

We got to the airport in plenty of time and had a couple of beers to round off the trip. Well, when I say a couple of beers, I mean five or six. Or was it seven? Anyway, by the time we were boarding the plane, needless to say we were fairly pissed.

It was quite unusual at the time, but it was a male steward, called Nigel according to his name badge, that greeted us at the door and, from the look on his face, he was not impressed with me and my bestie. We staggered to our seats and started arguing about who got the window seat.

Gary was always good at the high jump at school and clearly hadn't lost the knack, and so he won the argument by launching himself over the armrests and into the prized seat. Not before, however, ricocheting off the seat in front and knocking the Akubra off a particularly large and angry looking fellow passenger. Gary hit his target and fell immediately into a drunken sleep. How does he do that?

For some reason only known to himself, 'Mr Angry' grabbed *me* by my T-shirt and pulled me in so that we were nose to nose.

"If you do that again, I'll shove this bloody hat so far up your arse that you'll be chewing on it!" he growled, spitting the words through clenched teeth.

I figured it was best not to point out my innocence or the fact that his hat may, shall we say, get soiled in the process of his assault. No, as my dad always used to say, "Dunna poke an angree bear unless ya've got a bluddy death wish, mi bonny lad." Pretty clever was my dad, and so I decided not to poke the bear but slip ever-so-carefully into the aisle seat.

My mate Gazza, however, wasn't finished yet and, apart from talking in his sleep, which was very revealing about what he and Marlene had been up to (or perhaps what he'd like them to be up to), he kept farting. Farting loud and with an obnoxious stink that quickly attracted the attention of other passengers. Luckily, Mr Angry had fallen asleep, but it wasn't long before complaints had brought our friend Nigel to investigate.

Shrugging my shoulders and pointing at Gary, I slowly nodded my head in agreement with Nigel who was by now covering his nose and mouth with his handkerchief, I silently confirmed that this was indeed dreadfully disagreeable.

"Has your friend shat himself?" queried the steward with a serious but disgusted look on his face.

"Er, I, I don't know him. Just happen to be sitting next to him," I said untruthfully and with a haughty note in my voice. "I think he might have though, you know, shat himself that is."

These were the only things I could think of on the spur of the moment, and I wasn't sure what was coming next from old Nigel, now was I?

With the help of a female crew member, Nigel rather roughly escorted a bleary eyed and yawning Gary to the toilet and stood guard outside whilst my bestie dutifully managed to rid himself of the results of last night's vindaloo and the six Emu Bitters at the airport.

Once vacated, an 'Out of Order' sign was attached to the toilet door to save any poor unsuspecting passenger from a fate worse than death. A very wise move, as I knew well from bitter experience, but the stink still managed to permeate the air around the back ten rows or so. Poor buggers.

We disembarked in Perth where my dad collected us. He enquired where my van was and so I filled him in on our adventures on the Nullarbor. He didn't seem impressed.

Anyway, we dropped Gary off at his place, and I gave him a wave and shouted a "See ya later, Gazza!" from the open passenger window. As he entered his front door, he turned to face me, thumped his heart with his right fist and then pointed at me whilst mouthing the words, "Love ya mate, you're the best." He'd never done that before but, hey, he was only just sober and, maybe, it was because of the stoke from our epic trip.

I soon found out that I was way off the mark.

Little did I know that it would be the last time I saw him for quite some time. Things had changed without me realising it. I guess the signs were there, but I'd been too focused on our trip and too stoked with the surfing to notice, but it hit me like a train in the weeks after we got back to Perth.

Basically, Gary disappeared off the face of the earth, well my part of the planet anyway. The newly discovered love of his life, Marlene, had sucked him up like a vacuum cleaner and Gary was nowhere to be seen.

Gone were the nights at the pub sharing embellished stories of our surfing exploits, interspersed with planning our forays into the world of Perth's night life. No more competing for the attention of the girls we knew, or we were trying to get to know. Gone were the mid-week catch ups, just to hang out. Gone were the weekends surfing in Mandurah and beyond.

He was off on a new adventure of his own, and without me by his side. He had a new sidekick now, and she filled something in Gary's soul that I couldn't match. My best mate was head over heels in love with the girl of his dreams.

I guess that this moment was inevitable but, at first, I struggled to come to terms with the new norm. Both our worlds had been turned upside down but for different reasons. It took a while, but I began to realise that this was the right thing for Gary because he was happy in a way that he hadn't been before, and that's all that really mattered.

Maybe I had to find my own 'Marlene' so that I could sample some of that deep happiness and experience the highs and lows that love's journey brings. Perhaps I would one day.

I'm told that, eventually, it happens to All Surfers, Great and Small.

Epilogue – Cowabunga!

It seemed incredible that me and Gary could drift apart so completely.

I mean, we'd grown up together since that first day we met in high school, sitting side by side and taking on the formidable Mrs Dobson. And side by side is how we were thereafter.

We'd had many amazing adventures together, at home and overseas, almost too many to count. We'd surfed places around Australia and around the world; stood shoulder to shoulder against aggressive locals; against the angry fathers of girls we tried to seduce (or who tried to seduce us!); against officialdom, bouncers, and bullies. We'd faced our fears together and lived to tell the tale.

I suppose that sums it up. We'd lived, surfed, laughed, and loved together. Well, maybe not loved exactly—but there was that time on the beach at Yallingup in the pitch dark with those two girls from the campsite, but that's another story!

The weeks turned into months with no contact between us and then, out of the blue, Gary called me and said he was getting married. I couldn't believe it! Gary, married? But Cupid's arrow had pierced my mate's heart good and proper.

Marlene had cast her spell and tamed Gary who was now ready to do the 'Walk of Life', as Dire Straits were to sing some years later.

I was his best man of course and other than a couple of hiccups, it was, up to that point, one of the proudest moments of my life.

Despite our drunken promises at the end of the evening to keep in touch, we drifted even further apart. Gary and Marlene set up house in Perth's northern suburbs, and I pursued my dream to live by the beach in Mandurah.

Along the way, I met Samantha, a beautiful, blonde, ball of fire who quite literally swept me off my feet.

You see, I'd taken to skateboarding from my place to the bus station to get into work, and the coastal path took me almost half the way there. Every morning, the Indian Ocean would tug at my heart strings as I skated down the newly laid bitumen ribbon.

On one particular morning, I'd fixed my eyes on a beautiful set wave that was peeling off the reef at Blue Bay. My mind's eye carved turn after turn on that perfect wall of glass. As if in that dream, I carved a tight turn on my skateboard around a sharp bend in the path, not seeing the girl who was straight ahead. She saw me though and deftly side-stepped the impending collision.

To make sure that I learned a good lesson from the near disaster, just at the right moment, she stuck out her elbow and flicked me clean off my skateboard. I flew through the air in what seemed like slow motion, and ended up on my back in a bush, groaning in pain.

After first of all letting me know in plain language what she thought of my speed-skating antics, she must have taken pity on me because her expression softened and she came to my aid. My shoulder hurt, my neck hurt, my back hurt, and I'd scraped my hand along the gravel as I skidded off the path, and this was now bleeding profusely. I was in a pretty bad way.

"Are you OK?" she asked with just a hint of an accent. It was the voice of an angel. I mumbled something incomprehensible, and I let out a nervous laugh. Where was my wingman when I needed him?

The next few months were a beautiful blur of me and Samantha gradually falling in love. I say gradually, but I knew the minute she spoke to me on that beach path that *I* was in love.

Perhaps that's how Gary felt when he first spotted Marlene.

A wedding and many years of happy married life lay ahead for me and Samantha.

I became a departmental manager and finally earned a decent salary; we had three beautiful kids, two girls and a boy; and we moved to Fremantle to be closer to Sam's mum. This helped Sam juggle all this whilst qualifying as a para-legal, specialising in property settlements.

Life's been good, very good.

I completely lost touch with Gary but, fortunately, Chaz and I kept up a decent, if sporadic, friendship. He'd also settled in Mandurah, married a local girl called Wendy, and finished up with his own electrical business, riding on the back of the mining boom in Western Australia and the multiple property booms that followed.

We caught up for a surf from time to time, and these occasions gradually increased as our families grew up and our spare time increased. He was at the christening of our kids, and I was at his. We didn't live in each other's pockets, but I think we both needed to keep that connection to the past. A connection to those golden days that we didn't want to let slip into oblivion and be lost forever

Sometimes, we'd not see each other for four or five weeks, but then when we did get together, we'd give each other a quick nod and pick up the conversation as if it was only yesterday.

Funny how that happens with true friends, don't you think?

Unbeknown to me, Gary had recently moved to Rockingham, a few miles up the highway from me and, by chance, he bumped into Chaz when they both paddled out at a nearby surf break one sunny spring morning.

We both passed a few messages through Chaz and then eventually organised to have a three way get together for a surf in our old stomping ground around Falcon Bay.

That was well over fifteen years ago and, in large part thanks to our mate Chaz, me and Gary are now fully reunited. Much older, much greyer and, we hope, much wiser but still with that grommet-like stoke that 'straights' just don't understand.

Yep, me and Gary, and the new kid on the block, Chaz, The Three Musketeers, now well and truly ride again—and long may it continue. Cowabunga!

Acknowledgements

My sincere thanks to my surfing buddies who, along with my own cherished memories, provided a number of typically tall stories of their exploits, as well as recollections of true (if not sometimes a trifle exaggerated) events, the grains of all of which I sprinkled throughout the stories.

Last, and by no means least, my thanks to my good mates that I named as Ben and Gary in these ramblings. You know who you are, and I'm forever in your debt for your friendship, and for keeping me stoked and still surfing well past the age that most have retreated to their rocking chairs.

Thanks guys and I'll see you out the back at our favourite break the next time Huey smiles on us.

Glossary

1. ARVO – Australian slang for afternoon

2. BARREL / TUBE – When a wave spills over to form a tube that the skilled surfer can surf through

3. BLOW-IN – An unwelcome stranger at a surf break

4. BOARDIES – Surfing shorts

5. COWABUNGA! – Exclamation used by older surfers

6. CUT BACK – A surfing maneuver whereby the surfer turns the surfboard to head in the opposite direction

7. DAKS – Australian slang for trousers

8. DECK PLUG – A removable plug in the deck of old-fashioned hollow surfboards used to drain water ingress from the board

9. DINKIE DIE – A true Australian

10. DRONGO – Australian slang for idiot

11. DUNNY /DUNNIES – The bathroom / toilet(s)

12. FOOTY – Australian Rules Football

13. GLASSIE – Australian slang term for a glass collector in a pub or hotel

14. GOING OVER THE FALLS – When the surfer is thrown over by the lip of the breaking wave

15. GROMS / GROMMETS – Kids / young surfers just starting out

16. HAOLE – Hawaiian expression for a foreigner

17. HOBIE BOARDS – Surfboards made by Hobie Alter, a famous Californian board shaper / manufacturer in the 1960s and 1970s

18. HUARACHE SANDALS – Popular surf wear in the 1960s and 1970s

19. HUEY – The (fictitious) surf god

20. JOCKS – Slang term for male underpants

21. KICK OUT – A maneuver at the end of surfing a wave which positions the board and rider ready to paddle back out into the Line-Up

22. KNEE PADDLE – Kneeling up on the surfboard and paddling with both arms

23. KOOK – A derogatory term for a novice or

incompetent surfer

24. LINE-UP – The area of a surf break where surfers line up to take their turn to ride waves

25. NOGGIN – Slang word for head / skull

26. OUT THE BACK – Farther out than the breaking waves

27. PASH – Kissing passionately

28. PC PLOD – A slang term for a police officer on the beat

29. PIPELINE – A famous Hawaiian surfing location so called because the waves spill over the surfer's head, creating a tunnel that highly skilled surfers surf through, emerging at the end of the 'tube' before the wave collapses

30. POM / POMMIE – Australian slang word for a British person / people

31. ROCKERS – Youth subculture centred on motorcycles, rock 'n' roll music, and a tough, rebellious image

32. ROCKER SURFBOARD – The lengthways curve of a surfboard from nose to tail

33. ROOT / ROOTING – Australian slang for having sex

34. RSL – Returned and Services League / Australian Armed Forces Veterans Association

35. SERVO – Petrol / Gas Station

36. SET – A group of waves, several waves one after another

37. SET WAVE – The best wave in a set of waves

38. SHOULDER – The unbroken part of a wave close to the breaking section

39. SKEG – The fin at the back of a surfboard that gives stability and turning capability

40. SKIMPIES – Bikini-clad bar staff

41. SKULL (a drink) – Gulp down / drink quickly

42. SNEAKER SET – An unexpected set of large waves that catch surfers off guard

43. STOKED – Excited

44. TEN POUND POMS – British migrants encouraged to move to Australia after WW2 through to the 1970s and, with the support of the Australian Government, paying only ten pounds sterling per person for their passage to Australia

45. THE FLYING KANGAROO – Qantas Airways

46. THE POINT – A point of land at many beaches that can create near-perfect surfing waves

47. THE SANDALS – Famous surf music band that recorded the music over several surf movies, including the famous 'The Endless Summer' by Bruce Brown

48. THONGS – Australian name for flip-flop style

footwear

49. TUBE – Same as Barrel

50. TUCKER – Australian slang for food

51. ULUS / ULUWATU – Famous big wave surf break in Bali

52. WAHINE – Hawaiian for girl

53. WATCH HOUSE – Detention center at the main police station

54. WAX – Surf wax that is applied to the top surface of a surfboard to make it non-slip

55. WINTERSTICK – The predecessor of the snowboard, which was invented in the USA in the 1970s